THE
OFFENDERS

Center Point
Large Print

Also by Giles A. Lutz and available from
Center Point Large Print:

The Hardy Breed
The Golden Land
Wild Runs the River
The Grudge

**This Large Print Book carries the
Seal of Approval of N.A.V.H.**

THE
OFFENDERS

GILES A. LUTZ

CENTER POINT LARGE PRINT
THORNDIKE, MAINE

This Center Point Large Print edition is published
in the year 2015 by arrangement with
Golden West Literary Agency.

The text of this Large Print edition is unabridged.
In other aspects, this book may vary
from the original edition.
Printed in the United States of America
on permanent paper.
Set in 16-point Times New Roman type.

ISBN: 978-1-62899-634-0 (hardcover)
ISBN: 978-1-62899-639-5 (paperback)

Library of Congress Cataloging-in-Publication Data

Lutz, Giles A.
  The offenders / Giles A. Lutz. — Center Point Large Print edition.
    pages cm
  Summary: "Colonel Jefferson Karnes rode into Gallatin, Missouri, to
find out what was going on between the Gentiles and Mormons there.
Feelings were strong on both sides, and his hopes for a peaceful
solution are crushed with violence"—Provided by publisher.
  ISBN 978-1-62899-634-0 (hardcover : alk. paper)
  ISBN 978-1-62899-639-5 (pbk. : alk. paper)
  1. Large type books. I. Title.
  PS3562.U83O36 2015
  813′.54—dc23
                                                        2015016651

THE
OFFENDERS

CHAPTER 1

Gallatin, Missouri, was anything but an imposing town. There weren't over forty houses in the community, and the half-dozen stores should be more than enough to serve the needs of the surrounding country. The road, leading into town, was wet from a recent rain and heavily rutted. The false bright promise of Indian summer was over, and October had turned chilly and wet. Jefferson Karnes regarded a Missouri October with a jaundiced and apprehensive eye. She was a fickle jade, leading one on with her alluring, soft smiles. Without warning, she could turn into a vicious bitch, her fangs showing in the pelting rains, her claws in the raking north winds.

Jeff shivered as a new blast of wind wrapped around him. If the last week of adverse weather was any prophet, this northwestern part of Missouri was in for a long, hard, wet winter. Jeff hated excessive moisture in winter. The bottom dropped out of the roads, making traveling difficult if not impossible. When the roads froze, the conditions changed, but they weren't any better. The ruts then became hard and deep. A stumble or careless step could demand a fearful price of a human's or animal's leg.

If his grandmother were still alive, she would

7

berate him for this kind of thinking. She believed in looking on the bright side until optimism became a habit of life. In this case, Granny was wrong. Missouri winters had taught him that a pessimist was right far more often than an optimist.

He stopped his horse at the outskirts of the town. He wasn't sure what he was going to do, or how he would go about it. If Sam Turner didn't have a suggestion, Jeff didn't know which way he would turn.

Damn Aleck Doniphan, he thought in sudden wrath, for assigning him this task. If Doniphan were beside him, he would have given him pure hell. A grin twitched at Jeff's lip corners, then slowly spread. He would do nothing of the sort. Even if he did, he knew how Doniphan would accept such a tirade. He would throw back his massive head and roar with delight. That flow of laughter would sweep away all of Jeff's resentment. Jeff would do whatever Doniphan wanted him to do. When another had saved your life, you tried to please him.

A faint, sad-sweet cry drifted down from the skies. Jeff scanned the lowering clouds. He had to look hard before he located the flock of wild geese. He sat watching the V wend its way always southward until it was out of sight. He felt a vague nostalgia he couldn't name, a sense of something denied him.

He tried to put the fumbling thought into words. "Damned, if I don't wish I was going with you," he muttered. Geese were smarter than man. They knew enough to get out of a hostile climate.

He rubbed his eyes and rolled his shoulders before he picked up the reins. "Rowdy, it's not much of a town, but maybe we can find you shelter and something to eat."

The stallion flicked its ears backward and forward, as though he understood.

Gallatin was the county seat of Daviess. This was the place to pick up knowledge, for eventually every word of gossip, each serious bit of information would be exchanged in these stores and on these streets. Doniphan wanted information of what was going on in Daviess and Caldwell counties, and he expected Jeff to bring it to him.

Maybe this time, I'll bring him nothing, Jeff thought dourly. Doniphan was due to stub his toe. He won't, Jeff thought in resignation. Doniphan had an old hound's nose when it came to smelling out and separating fact from rumor. When Jeff finished his report, Doniphan could say with some certainty just what was going on in the two counties.

"That damned Doniphan," Jeff said, but he was smiling, and there was admiration in his tone.

He made his way down the street, riding slouched over, paying little attention to the people he saw. But they paid attention to him. A stranger always drew interest.

His slouching detracted from his height. After Doniphan, he was the tallest man in the Missouri Volunteers, and he lacked a full two inches of Doniphan's height. His posture made him look like a bag of bones, carelessly assembled. He looked to be all nobs and odd angles. A casual observer would put Jefferson Karnes down as clumsy and unco-ordinated, but that would be a false assumption. When fancy or need struck Jeff, he could move with surprising speed and precision. His face was long and angular and when he was absorbed in thought, he reminded one of a mournful hound. His nose was large and bony, the most prominent of his features. His jaw was square and widely hinged to move that large mouth. A smile or a laugh could completely change his appearance, filling his face with warmth. He was on the lee side of his thirty years, and as yet he had found no woman he wished to be bound to permanently. He was in no hurry. One of these days, a laughing pair of eyes would ensnare him. He would cope with that when it happened.

His first inkling of trouble was the bunching of Rowdy's muscles and the frightened snort from the stallion. Out of the corner of his eye he saw a tawny form spring at his left side.

He tried to do several things at once. He kicked

the left boot from its stirrup, sawed frantically on the reins, and tried to dig under his outer coat for his gun. He had a confused impression of flashing teeth in an animal that probably wasn't as big as it seemed. My God, he thought in instant alarm, this damned town's got wolves roaming its main street.

He kicked out with his left boot. His aim wasn't accurate, for he didn't make contact. Those teeth fastened into his boot at the ankle, clamping there with the force of a vise.

He yelled as he tried to kick off the dangling, threshing weight. Rowdy went into a paroxysm of terror. He bugled his fear and bounded sideways.

Rowdy's unexpected move unseated Jeff. He went down, landing hard on his side in the muddy street. His teeth jarred together, and he felt the clammy touch of mud on his face. He gained something from the fall; the dog let go of him.

He sat up, trying to wipe mud from his face. He got the pistol out, and his head whipped about, looking for the attacker. He caught a glimpse of the tawny form as it dashed between two buildings. The dog was out of sight before Jeff could aim at him. He looked down the street and swore. Rowdy was racing out of town. He would keep at it until he outran his fear, or until he became exhausted.

Jeff swore with all the outrage he felt. If he only could have had one clear shot at that damned dog. He looked at his boot. The animal's teeth hadn't torn through the leather, but they had scarred the boot, marking the considerable span of the dog's jaws.

He looked around at laughter. It came from the three men standing under the tin awning of the store across the street. Two of them towered in height over the third one, but all of them shared the same enjoyment of what they had just seen. They slapped their thighs and mauled each other with open-handed slaps. Every now and then, one of them would point at Jeff again, and the laughter would break out afresh.

Jeff clambered slowly to his feet. He surveyed the muddy damage to his clothing. He could do nothing about that at the moment. His jaws were set so hard they ached. He crossed the street with deliberate steps, still carrying the gun in his hand.

The small man first noticed Jeff's approach. His laughter died out uneasily, and wariness filled his eyes. He gulped and said something to the other two that Jeff was too far away to catch.

Their laughter ceased, but ribald mirth still twitched at their lips. A mock sobriety was on the faces of the bigger men, and one of them said with false solicitousness, "Mister, I sure hope you ain't hurt. You came down off that horse awful fast. Is that the best way to get out of a saddle?"

His laughter poured forth again. He lacked three

inches of Jeff's height, and too much of his weight was fat.

He caught his breath and gasped, "Mace, did you see the way he landed? When he hit, he splattered like a fresh cow pancake on a hot rock. Funniest thing I ever saw."

"I saw it, Hamp," Mace responded. Hamp's uncontrollable laughter built up Mace's humor afresh. He was a shade taller than Hamp, but there was little fat about him. His features were chiseled hard, and that solidly packed body gave the impression of power. His eyes were slate-colored and equally as cold.

Jeff waited patiently for them to stop laughing. His expression didn't change, though the muscles along the jaw line tightened. He said in a conversational tone, "When you clowns get through enjoying yourselves, I've got something to say to you."

The small man hadn't joined in the laughter this time. His pinched cheeks were pale, and his nervousness was apparent. He sensed something dangerous in the big stranger that the other two had missed entirely.

Mace's laugh cut off in mid-note. His eyes narrowed, and his nostrils pinched together with the increased rush of his breathing.

Jeff looked calmly at Mace. Mace's hands bunched. Here was a sensitive man, quick to accept affront. Hamp was a thick dolt, for if he heard what Jeff said, the words didn't register. Between whoops of laughter he managed to gasp, "Did you see the way ole Devil took him out of his saddle, Mace? You taught Devil well to go after strangers."

Mace flashed Hamp a warning glance, but it was too late. "So you're the owner of that goddamned dog," Jeff said softly.

"What if I am?" he challenged.

Jeff's voice picked up no heat. "I don't believe in disciplining another man's dog. But you haven't got an ordinary dog. I wouldn't give him any more consideration than I would a rabid wolf. The next time I see him, I'll blow his head off."

Mace paled, and he sucked in his breath. "The hell you will." He choked over his words. "I trained him to go after strangers. I want that kind of protection."

Jeff studied him so long that it was an open affront. "That puts a new value on the whole thing. If I see you with him again, I'll have to decide which to shoot first. If I pick the one with the least brains, that would have to be you, wouldn't it?"

Mace's face turned livid. "Nobody talks to me like that without it earning them a lesson."

"You'd better start teaching," Jeff said.

"Mace, he's holding a gun," the short man yelped.

"I see it, Nobby," Mace snarled. "I'm not worried."

At least he was concerned, for his face had turned white, except for twin spots of color burning at the cheekbones.

"If that's bothering you," Jeff said easily. He slipped the gun into his coat pocket. "Get at your lesson, mister."

Mace licked his lips, and his eyes darted uneasily to his companions. Indecision was written all over his face. Should he take this stranger by himself and see how he fared, or call in his cronies from the start.

A wicked spark danced in Jeff's eyes. If Mace called the other two in, the odds wouldn't bother him. It would only make the brawl last a little longer; the ultimate result a little more difficult.

Maybe he should take off the hampering over-coat before Mace made his move. Before he could decide, a voice behind him roared, "What the hell's going on here?"

CHAPTER 2

Jeff whirled and looked at the short, blocky figure, standing in the doorway of the store. The speaker's face was wrathful, the outthrust jaw belligerent.

"I'll be damned," Jeff said. "Sam Turner." He

laughed with pure delight. Turner was his main reason for riding to Gallatin, but he hadn't expected to find him so easily.

"Jeff Karnes." Turner sounded as though he couldn't believe his eyes. "What did you do? Lose your way?"

He lacked a full head of reaching Jeff's height, but he had a massive span of shoulders. His arms were long and powerful. His blue eyes could be friendly, or crackle with hostility.

"Jeff," he roared, and lumbered toward Jeff. He lifted him off the ground with effortless ease. He whirled about, his mouth open with uproarious laughter.

Jeff beat Turner on the top of his head with his fists. His mouth was open too, but not from laughter. He gasped for breath against the pressure on his ribs.

"You trying to break my ribs?" he wheezed.

Turner set him down. "You never could endure very much."

Jeff drove a fist into Turner's shoulder. Most men would have staggered under the blow, but not Turner. Jeff might as well have tried to knock the store off its foundation.

They stood beaming at each other. Turner lifted his arms again, and Jeff retreated.

"Sam," he begged. "Don't show me any more how glad you are to see me."

"See that ugly face," Turner jeered. "It took all

this time to get it out of my mind. Now I'll be having nightmares again." Jeff grinned. They had spent eight years of their childhood together. "I shouldn't have moved away. You had a little respect then."

"For you," Turner hooted, "never."

He must have recalled something, for he frowned heavily. He whirled on the three who had been ready to jump Jeff.

"What the hell was going on here?" he demanded.

The three seemed a little bewildered at the display of affection between Turner and this stranger.

"Mace, Hamp, answer me," Turner said impatiently. He ignored the small one.

"He rides in here too damned clumsy to stay on his horse," Mace growled. "Then the big, tough man blames everybody but himself."

The tightness returned to Jeff's face. "Tell it the way it was," he snapped.

"Jeff, you tell me," Turner invited.

"This half-wild dog jumped me. Grabbed me around the ankle and spooked Rowdy. Rowdy made a quick move and dumped me. From what I hear, this"—he jerked his thumb at Mace—"owns the damned dog. He ran before I could get a shot at him."

Mace's face blackened anew. "If you ever try to shoot him—" he started.

17

"You'll do what?" Turner interrupted coldly. "I'm sick and tired of you keeping that dog around. I told you before, if he bit anybody else, I was going to do something about it." He glanced at Jeff. "Jeff, you've got my permission to shoot that dog when you see it again."

"Just a goddamned minute," Mace Nixon howled. "Nobody takes that kind of liberties with my dog."

"I just did," Turner said harshly.

The savagery showed in Mace's pinched face and hollowed his cheeks. His words ran together, and he had to slow them down to make himself coherent. "Ever since you pinned on that tin badge you been strutting around like you're the second coming of Christ. By God, I'm telling you—"

"You want to try and change things right now?" Turner asked.

Mace's eyes went from Turner to Jeff, then he looked at Hamp and Nobby. Apparently, he did some mental evaluating, and he didn't like the figure he came up with.

"I'll pick my own time," he said sullenly.

"Get out of here," Turner said in disgust.

Mace swept him with a furious glance, then turned and stalked down the street. The other two hurried to catch up with him. Nobby said something to Mace that Jeff and Turner couldn't catch, but they heard Mace's reply.

18

"Just keep your damned mouth shut," Mace yelled.

"A thoroughly pleasant individual," Jeff drawled.

"He can do anything he wants with them. It doesn't stop them from tagging at his heels. He's a loudmouth with too much standing and authority. So far, nobody's taught him the right lesson. I feel like volunteering for that job right now."

Jeff still watched the three. "Who are they?" he asked with idle curiosity.

"Farmers. Mace Nixon is the only successful one. His Pa left him a good-sized piece of land. He's smart enough to work at that farm. Hamp Inman and Nobby Owens are damned near the shiftless class. They've both got little piddling pieces of land. They'll work enough to keep their bellies from getting too empty, but that's about all."

"I'm surprised that Nixon tolerates them," Jeff said. Usually a successful, hard-working man had no time for the likes of Inman and Owens.

Turner smiled sardonically. "Nixon doesn't want to lose anybody in his militia company."

That explained a lot of things. "Oh hell," Jeff said. "One of those things." If an individual had enough money to outfit and uniform a militia company, he automatically was the commanding officer. It was a sure way to buy authority and power.

Turner chuckled at Jeff's reaction. "You picking on Nixon? You're a militia man yourself."

Jeff was, but he didn't work at it any more. He had never resigned, but he was no longer active. Not too far in the past militia companies were a necessity. But that was in the days when the men of a community had to band together for the mutual protection of their families. That need was fading. The threat of an Indian attack was about gone. The militia still had a powerful attraction for most men. They could dress up in their uniforms and parade around their home town, playing soldier without any real danger. Meeting nights were a good excuse to get away from home. Men could spend those nights sitting around drinking and talking. No wonder the militia was so popular.

Jeff grinned. "I guess I didn't treat him with enough respect. That makes him a captain, doesn't it?"

Turner spat into the mud. "It does. And he never lets Gallatin forget it. Wait until you see Nixon's outfit. You wouldn't believe it. He calls them the Delaware Amaraguns. They wear full Indian dress down to the feathers in their hair. They whoop and carry on like actual savages."

Jeff shook his head in disbelief. "What does Amaragun mean?"

"Who knows?" Turner asked wearily. "You better get out of those muddy clothes."

"I've got to pick up my horse first. He ran when Nixon's dog spooked him."

"I'm still saddled, Jeff. I'll go out and catch him."

"I'd appreciate that," Jeff said warmly. "Where's a hotel?"

"In Gallatin?" Turner hooted. "I think you can get a room at Ma Gibson's boardinghouse." He pointed out the boardinghouse. "Her food couldn't be better. I know. I live there. You still riding Warrior?"

A tinge of sadness was in Jeff's smile. "We hate to admit we're getting old, Sam. Warrior's dead. I'm riding his son. He's a young replica of his sire."

"Aw," Turner said in instant sorrow. "I hate to hear that. Warrior was some horse."

Jeff had spent all of his grief over Warrior some time ago. "He was getting pretty old, Sam. He left most of his good traits in Rowdy."

"I'd better go look him up," Turner said, and plodded toward a horse tied to a hitch rack.

Jeff watched him go, his face softened with affection. Doniphan told him that Turner had been elected sheriff six months ago. "It couldn't have happened to a better man," Jeff muttered as he turned to walk toward the boardinghouse.

He scrubbed his boots on the gunny bags laid before the door. This weather was the despair of a woman, particularly if she was a good housekeeper. This was the best job he could do on cleaning his boots.

He knocked on the door. Somebody must have been standing very near it, for he heard the knob turn immediately. The door opened, and a pleasant-faced, plump woman looked at him.

"Yes?" she asked. Her eyes widened as they ran over him. "You're Jefferson Karnes?"

He knew he had never seen this woman before. "You're right," he admitted. "But how did you know?"

His confusion amused her, for her eyes crinkled before she laughed. Her laugh was a delight to hear, rich and musical. "Were you beginning to believe I was a sorceress?"

"Something like that," he confessed.

Her laugh showed beautiful, white teeth. She thrust out a hand. "I'm Alverna Gibson. Sam's told me a lot about you. How could I fail to know you?"

He took the hand and smiled. "I'm sorry to bring all this mud into your house. I was hoping you have a room."

"I have. You can't help the mud. Isn't this weather terrible? I'm afraid this will be a bad winter."

His smile deepened. She was comfortable to know. "I'm afraid you're right." He thought she was around forty. Gray was streaking that magnificent red hair, but the green eyes were still clear and unfaded. Though she was now plump, it wasn't hard to imagine what a stunning woman she must have been twenty years ago.

She heard the footsteps coming down the stairs before he did, for she looked past him and said, "Delight, you've heard Sam speak of Mr. Karnes. Now I want you to meet him."

Jeff turned. A girl came slowly down the steps. She was wand-slender and graceful, moving with the poetic beauty of a meandering stream. He knew these two had to be mother and daughter. He felt breathless, and there was a huge hollow in his stomach. He had seen eye-arresting women before, but this one was a step ahead of all of them.

CHAPTER 3

Mrs. Gibson's next words confirmed Jeff's assumption, for she said, "Mr. Karnes, I want you to meet my daughter, Delight."

Jeff was afraid he gaped like a schoolboy. He would place this girl around seventeen or eighteen. She knew the effect she had on men, for an impish gleam danced in her eyes.

"I have heard of you, Mr. Karnes," she murmured as she extended a hand. "But after listening to Sam, I thought you would be at least nine feet tall."

He realized she mocked him. "Ah," he said. He enclosed her hand in his big paw. "Sam exaggerates."

"Maybe he doesn't. He says you did nothing but order him around."

She tried to tug her hand free, but he wouldn't release it. She had a clever, mocking tongue, and she deserved some kind of rebuff.

"I've shrunk some since then," he said easily. He stared at her, forcing her to look away first. That uneven rhythm was still in his heart. She had her mother's coloration. She looked like an April morning after a long and wearying winter. A master craftsman had sculptured her face.

He was satisfied with the faint blush his scrutiny caused and grinned and released her hand.

He had thrown her into confusion. She was probably used to having the upper hand with men, and he had taken her aback. Give her two or three more years, he thought, and she would truly be an awesome menace.

"I'm very happy to meet you, Delight," he said softly.

She tried to regain her aplomb. She wrinkled her nose and shrugged. "Oh, that silly name. My father gave it to me. Ma refuses to let me change it."

"Your father is a man of great wisdom," Jeff said.

She tried to return his gaze, and she couldn't.

Her confusion had increased. Jeff had her on the run. He intended to keep her that way.

He turned his head to smile at Mrs. Gibson. Was that a speculative regard in her eyes? He wondered if she disapproved of his exchange with her daughter.

He wanted to soften Mrs. Gibson's speculation, and he said, "May I see the room please?"

For a moment, he had the horrible fear she would change her mind, then she slowly nodded.

"Delight, did you finish cleaning that room?" she asked.

"Almost," the girl said. She looked Jeff over, taking in his muddy clothes. The gleam came back to her eyes. She had found a way to sting him in return for putting her on the defensive. "Though it won't stay that way long. Not if he doesn't quit rolling in the mud."

Jeff felt his cheeks burn. He glanced involuntarily at his clothes. He did present a sorry spectacle, and was tempted to explain what had happened. He let the impulse fade. He wasn't going to explain anything to her and give her the impression he sought favor in her eyes.

"Delight," Mrs. Gibson reproved her daughter.

Delight laughed. She had the same rich, warm tones of her mother. "I'll finish the room right away, Ma," she said. A triumphant glance swept Jeff, then she turned and climbed the stairs, her head carried high.

"I apologize for her," Mrs. Gibson said. "Each year she grows more—" She hesitated, trying to find words to express herself.

"Sure of herself?" he offered. "That's understandable. Don't apologize for her. She is well and properly named."

Mrs. Gibson shook her head, half in disagreement with what he said and half in gratitude. "She gets her way too often. People go out of their way to please her. It is difficult to raise a daughter alone."

So Mrs. Gibson was a widow. Jeff nodded in sober understanding. Delight had a rare beauty, and it was only normal for her to expect tribute to it. But that expectation could become a demand. Jeff could appreciate how Mrs. Gibson feared that.

"Her name is unusual," Mrs. Gibson said. "Her father was so pleased when she was born that he insisted upon naming her Delight. Two years later a fall from a horse killed him. He didn't live to see her grow up."

"He couldn't have picked a more fitting name," Jeff said promptly. This woman had been widowed early in life. Her struggle to make a living showed in the fine tracery of lines in her face. Jeff felt an instant liking and respect for her.

He started to say something when the opening of the door interrupted him. Turner came in, carrying Jeff's war bag. He smiled at Mrs. Gibson.

"Hello, Alverna. I sent you a disreputable-looking character, didn't I? But I've seen him look better. Honest. Do you have a room for him?"

She had a special liking for Turner, for her smile was easy and warm. "I'm grateful, Sam. Mr. Karnes didn't say how long he was going to stay."

At Turner's questioning look Jeff shrugged and said, "I don't know. Maybe a week. Maybe longer."

"Fine, fine," Turner approved. "I didn't have to chase Rowdy far. I guess the run in that mud wore him out. I thought I was looking at Warrior again. He came back without any fuss. Alverna, I put him in your shed."

"Good, Sam. Mr. Karnes, will you be here for supper?"

Jeff's stomach rumbled, reminding him how hungry he was. "I'd like nothing better."

She nodded. "Supper will be ready in an hour."

"That gives me time to get out of these muddy clothes." Jeff hesitated. "If my room is ready."

"It should be by now. It's the first room to the right at the head of the stairs."

"Thank you," Jeff returned.

She smiled and walked out of the hallway. Turner watched her until she turned a corner. "Fine woman."

Jeff didn't really know her, but he could agree. "She is that."

He walked up the stairs, Turner following him. Turner refused to let go of the war bag.

Delight came out of the room just as they approached.

"Delight," Turner said, "this is Jeff Karnes."

"I've already met him." That impish gleam danced in her eyes again. Jeff braced himself. The gleam told him she wasn't through trying to sting him.

"Though I'm a little disappointed, Sam," she went on.

Turner frowned. "How's that?"

"After you said so much about him I guess I expected to see something more than an ordinary muddy man. I would have thought he could walk in any mud without falling down."

Jeff sighed. "I guess my only salvation is for the mud to dry up. It's too late to train my clumsy feet."

She wrinkled her nose at him. Her faint smile said he had protected himself. She went toward the stairs with that beautiful, gliding movement.

Turner had quick perception. He waited a moment, then said, "You been clashing swords?"

"Something like that," Jeff admitted.

Turner saw that Jeff didn't intend to offer an explanation. He opened the door of the room and let Jeff enter first.

Jeff looked around the room with approval. It wasn't luxury, but it had all the comforts a man should ever want.

Turner sat down on the bed. "Didn't you tell Delight how that mud got all over you?"

Jeff shook his head. He opened his war bag and began pawing through it. "Just never got around to it." He pulled out a clean pair of pants, frowning at their wrinkled condition. He laid a fresh shirt beside them. He placed his shaving equipment beside the bowl and pitcher.

Turner started to rise. "I expect I could get some hot water from Alverna."

Jeff poured water into his shaving mug and worked up a lather. "This won't be the first time I've shaved in cold water."

Turner grinned. "As ornery as you were, I didn't think you'd ever grow up to shave at all."

Jeff exchanged smiles with Turner through the mirror. They had hundreds of shared reminiscences to talk over.

"Just as well you didn't tell Delight why Rowdy dumped you."

Jeff stopped the path of his razor. "Why not?"

Turner shrugged. "You'll find out soon enough."

There was no use prying at Turner. He would say only what he pleased about a subject.

"I'm glad to see you wearing that badge, Sam."

"Caught the voters in a weak moment." Turner sighed with mock woe. "I'll never make it again. By now, they've had enough time to know all about me." He grinned at Jeff's derisive snort. "You still in Liberty, Jeff?"

"Just outside it, Sam. I found the place I wanted."

Turner's eyes brightened. Jeff used to talk about nothing but raising horses, even when he was very young. "So that dream finally came true. Rowdy the kind of horses you're raising?"

Jeff scraped the lather off one cheek before he answered. "Right now, the best. But last year's crop promises to shove him to the back of the picture."

Turner lay back on an elbow. "I doubt that, Jeff. You see Aleck lately?"

"Occasionally," Jeff answered absently. "The militia and his law office keep him pretty busy." He shook his head in unconscious admiration. "I don't know how he keeps up with everything the way he does." Two years ago, he had brought Doniphan with him on a hunting trip. Turner had liked Doniphan almost at first sight. "Aleck still talks about that hunt with us."

"He sure showed me up," Turner grumbled. "I thought I was good, but he was the best wing shot I ever saw."

Jeff grinned. Sam had worked hard to outdo Doniphan, but he had failed. "You topped me," he said in consolation.

"That was never hard," Sam jeered.

"I was using one of your guns," Jeff said. "The sights were out of line."

"The hell they were," Turner spluttered. "That

was my best gun—" He broke off and grinned as he realized Jeff was stringing him. "I enjoyed Aleck's visit. I'd like to see him again."

"Maybe you will," Jeff said noncommittally. "By the way, Aleck was promoted to a brigadier general."

"They picked right," Turner grunted. "When you were here, you said something about you thought you had a promotion coming."

Jeff started changing his clothes. "I told you I wasn't very active."

His evasiveness warned Turner. "Ah, so you got it. Tell me what it is now so I'll know how much respect to give you."

Jeff grinned sheepishly. "Lieutenant colonel."

"That high?" Turner said in mock amazement. "If I wasn't so comfortable, I'd get up and bow down to the floor."

Jeff pulled up his pants and buttoned them. "If you did, I'd kick your ass."

"Why did Aleck send you up here?" Turner asked suddenly. It amused him to see Jeff look startled. "Hell, it just came to me there has to be some reason behind your trip."

Jeff sat down and put his boots back on. He stretched out his long legs and contemplated his boot toes. Turner was a sharp one.

"He sent me, Sam. You know the nose Aleck has when it comes to smelling out trouble. He thinks he smells more trouble. He loves this state.

He works his butt off to keep anything from happening to it."

He paused, reflecting on just where to start.

"Go on," Turner said impatiently.

"I guess I can't tell you anything about the Mormons. Governor Boggs split up Ray County to make Caldwell County to give the Mormons a place to settle. He was pretty stout in his belief that the Mormons are Americans too, even if they have a different religion."

"Go ahead," Turner said cautiously. A new tension seemed to have gripped him. "A strange, standoffish people. Maybe you know something new about them."

"Everybody was in favor of Boggs's proclamation after Independence drove the Mormons out. The Mormons are hard-working people with thrifty ways." Jeff smiled bleakly. "Such cussedness is bound to stir up a lot of resentment against them."

Doniphan had talked at length about the Mormons, and Jeff had listened attentively. He took a fresh breath and continued. "Boggs tried to prevent friction from breaking out again. The Mormons could have Caldwell County, but they couldn't own land outside it, unless two thirds of the people living in another county voted in their favor."

He realized he must be telling an old story to Turner. "Hell, you know more than I do about all this."

"Maybe." Turner still wasn't ready to talk. "What's got Aleck so upset?"

"Rumor that real trouble is building up fast around here. I asked him why he didn't just ask Boggs to order out the militia and stomp those rumors to death. He said Boggs hasn't heard of any such rumors. Boggs believes everything is sailing along smooth up here." He pointed a finger at Turner. "That's why Aleck sent me; to see how much talk and how much fact is behind those rumors."

The last vestige of humor faded from Turner's face. "Does Aleck think somebody could be stopping those reports of trouble from getting to Boggs?"

"He does," Jeff said promptly. "Cloyd Lucas."

Turner whistled softly. "General Lucas."

"One and the same," Jeff said dryly. "Also Secretary of State. He's in an ideal position to cut off every report of trouble from reaching Boggs."

Turner pulled on an ear lobe and scowled. "But why?"

"Who knows for sure?" Jeff asked wearily. "A relative of his was supposed to have been killed by the Mormons in Independence. Maybe he hates them enough to wipe them out of Missouri. It's well known that he's a jealous man. Maybe he resents Aleck's success. If he can keep the nit-picking from reaching Boggs until real trouble breaks out, then Boggs will be forced to call out

33

the militia. Lucas will lead it. It would make a big man of him."

Turner's hands bunched until the knuckles stood out starkly. "Why, the miserable bastard."

"Yes," Jeff said shortly. He didn't know Lucas too well, but he didn't need much contact to build a dislike for him.

"It's time to talk, Sam. I want to know everything you know about the Mormons. Even if you think some of your guesses are wild."

Turner's eyes looked haunted. "Jeff, it's gone far beyond the rumor stage. People are beginning to scream when will Boggs get off his fat ass and call out the militia? If he waits much longer, it can break into an open war. There's been a few clashes between the Mormons and gentiles. You know what a gentile is?"

"That's us," Jeff answered. "What the Mormons call a nonbeliever. Where does the fault lay for the trouble that's sprouting up, Sam?"

Turner threw up his hands. "Who can say. One does something that offends another. Getting even is the only thing that remains in the offended's mind. Both sides have stolen stock. Each new offense only ensures that it will get worse."

"Have any of the Mormons moved into Daviess County, Sam?"

"I know they have, though I couldn't point out exactly where they are. They keep the fact they're Mormon pretty well hidden. They know the

34

gentiles would burn them out some night." He made a wry face. "Damned if I can get used to that term. When I hear it, I don't think they're talking about me."

"Are both sides beyond listening to reason?"

Turner sighed. "Maybe not that far yet. But it's getting damned close. Would you expect a man like Nixon to use any reason. I've heard him yelling that the Mormons are worse than the locusts. The locusts eventually leave; the Mormons never." He looked woebegone. "Both sides are hardheaded. Mix cussedness with that, and you've got pure poison on your hands." Turner shook his head in slow admiration. "That damned old fox. Aleck got a smell of this without even coming up here."

"He knows human nature, Sam. He was familiar with that Independence trouble. Nothing has been changed. He suspects the same ingredients are being thrown in the same pot. What other kind of a stew would you expect?"

Turner swore softly. "Have you got anything to tell Aleck so far?"

Jeff shook his head. "Nothing definite. I'll stick around for a while and see what develops."

Turner stood and stretched. "I'm glad you're going to be here. Must be getting close to supper." He hesitated as though he changed his mind about saying something.

"Spit it out, Sam."

"No. It'll come out soon enough." Turner walked out of the room, and Jeff followed him.

They descended the stairs and turned toward the dining room. Just as they started to enter Delight came toward them.

She said in a cutting tone, "Sam, you don't know people very well. I never had any use for an animal abuser." She raked Jeff with hot, angry eyes before she moved away.

Jeff's mouth sagged. "What was that all about?"

Turner pointed at the long table inside the room. A dozen men were seated around. Nixon's loud talking made him the most prominent.

"He eats most of his evening meals here," Turner said in a low aside. "That's what I started to tell you up there. Then I hoped maybe he wouldn't be here tonight."

That didn't ease Jeff's bewilderment at all. "How does that explain Delight's—"

Turner cut him off with a disgusted glance. "Hell, haven't you seen it yet? She thinks Nixon is pretty close to wonderful. He's done some talking to her before we came down."

CHAPTER 4

Jeff alternately accused Delight and excused her. Was she so blind that she couldn't see that Nixon was a loudmouthed braggart? Jeff wanted to defend her. He had no doubt Nixon presented an entirely different face to her. Nixon was good-looking enough to attract a woman. In a town this small, he could even be outstanding. He was prosperous, and he had a meager amount of distinction. That didn't satisfy the anger in Jeff. If she couldn't see Nixon for what he was, there were other people who should have straightened her out. Alverna or Sam could have told her the truth about Nixon. He sighed at the fallacy of that reasoning. Alverna or Sam wouldn't get anywhere trying to talk to Delight. She wouldn't have listened to anything that was opposite to what she wanted to believe.

He swore at himself. This girl shouldn't be causing him this much distress. He had seen her three times, all of them brief. He couldn't be hit this hard. Maybe not, he argued. But something had happened to him. It had wrecked his appetite.

He toyed with his food until Turner asked, "Isn't it good?"

"Fine," Jeff tried to say heartily.

"You sure don't act like it. What's eating on you?"

"Just thinking of what you told me," Jeff lied.

Turner searched his face. "Well, it hasn't bothered my appetite. I never knew Alverna to serve a bad meal."

Jeff was relieved that Turner turned to his eating. He paid covert attention to Nixon. He should have smashed him when he first saw him. He groaned inwardly. Wouldn't that make him stand high in Delight's eyes? Nixon had lied about what had happened, or she wouldn't have displayed so much hostility toward Jeff.

Nixon dominated the talk around the table. He expressed his opinions on any subject in a loud, positive voice. Jeff writhed as he listened to him. Good God! All Delight had to do was to listen to take an accurate measurement of this loudmouth.

Delight helped Alverna serve the table. Each time she passed Nixon, she gave him a dazzling smile, or paused to say something to him. Nixon never lost an opportunity to pat her hand, or touch her arm.

That burned Jeff. You damned fool, he told himself. Quit watching them. He couldn't catch Delight's eyes. She treated him as though he didn't exist. He noticed that something was bothering Alverna. If somebody said anything to her that called for a laugh or a smile, she responded with a feeble and painful effort.

"Are you going to eat all night?" Jeff growled at Turner.

"Until I'm satisfied." Turner finished another cup of coffee, then stood. "Now I'm done."

Alverna caught up with them at the front door. She stopped Jeff with a hand on his arm.

"Jeff, I'm sorry," she whispered.

He tried to look astounded. "For what?"

She bit her lower lip in a surge of exasperation. "I wish she was young enough to spank. I saw the way she treated you. I also saw the way you ate."

Some of the despondency left Jeff. He wasn't alone. "It doesn't matter." His smile was almost sincere.

"It matters to me," Alverna said fiercely. "I overheard Mace tell her about you getting muddy. You abused his dog and forced it to attack you. If he hadn't been there, you would have shot it."

"He happens to be a damned liar," Jeff said levelly.

Her eyes flashed. "Don't you think I know that? Delight can't see beyond the end of her nose." She was a mother, and she couldn't help but defend her own daughter. "But she sees him in a different light, Jeff. He heaps favors on her. He makes her believe she's the most important woman in the world."

"Maybe she is to him."

"No," she said indignantly. "His kind never change. He'll do anything to get his way, then he's not the same. I think I'd shoot him myself before I'd let him break her heart."

Jeff took both of her hands. "Don't let it fret you too much. Something will happen to open her eyes."

She searched his face. "You know something already about him?"

He shook his head regretfully. "No more than that I don't like him. Right now, that's not enough. You keep your patience, you hear me?"

Her attempt at a smile was almost true. "Yes. It's done me a lot of good just to talk to you."

"Don't say anything to Delight." He chuckled. "She's down on me enough already."

He pressed her hands and stepped out of the door.

Turner followed him. "Alverna caught more of what was going on than I did," he grumbled. He cut his eyes at Jeff. "So that's why you didn't eat."

"I told you I wasn't hungry."

Turner's laughter said you're a damned poor liar. He walked a few steps in silence. "She's something."

"Yes," Jeff said curtly. He could talk to Alverna about Delight; he was in no mood to talk on the same subject to anybody else.

Turner started to say something, then his voice rose. "Look!"

Jeff turned his head. A pitiful file of people trudged through the mud of Gallatin's main street.

The mud made pushing the handcarts laborious and difficult work. The carts were piled high with family possessions. Women followed their men, carrying children too small to walk. Older children walked with their mothers, clutching at a skirt for support. If the boys were old enough, they pushed at the carts to help their fathers. Some of the older children carried bundles that couldn't go on the overcrowded carts.

"What the hell?" Seeing these people startled the words out of Jeff. They had turned themselves into no more than beasts of burden. "What are they doing?"

Turner spat into the mud before he answered. "Moving. Don't ask why they're not using horses and wagons. They can't afford them."

Jeff stared at the sorry procession. Their drooping shoulders and lagging feet said they had walked far today. It was already dark, and still they plodded on. Utter exhaustion stamped men's and women's faces, making them look far older than they were.

"They're going to stop in Gallatin for the night?" Jeff made a question out of it.

Turner shrugged. "I doubt it. I'll bet they can't scrape up the price of a single room between them. Where would they find anybody to put them up?"

Before Jeff could ask what Turner meant by the last remark, somebody came out of a building across the street. He stopped at the sight of the bone-weary people.

"Get out of here," he yelled wrathfully. "You're worse than the plague."

"Billings," Turner yelled in instant anger. "That's enough of that. Open your mouth again, and I'll shut it for you."

"I figured you'd think that way," Billings shouted.

"Why goddamn it!" Turner exploded. He started toward the figure.

Billings whipped about and ran down the street.

Turner stopped and muttered, "He's not worth running down. He only mouths off what Nixon thinks. He's one of Nixon's militia."

The people in the street had never paused nor turned their heads because of the yelling.

It told Jeff what they were. "They're Mormons."

Turner nodded. "Yes. I've seen a lot of them come through here. I'd say they're trying to make Far West in Caldwell County. Joseph Smith has designated Far West as their second Zion. He's supposed to have gotten those golden plates straight out of God's hands."

Jeff nodded. He was familiar with the founding of the Mormon belief. "Independence was Zion before they were run out."

"I guess Smith can call any place he wants to Zion. It's kinda scary when people believe so passionately in him."

42

Jeff could agree to that. "Have you ever been in Far West?"

"Once. I was tracking a horse thief. I barely got into town. Those people made it plain I wasn't welcome." Turner's face clouded at the memory. "I told them as long as they stayed where they belonged, I'd stay where I belonged. From the looks of the way things are going, I wasted my breath. I'll buy a drink, Jeff."

"I'll accept it."

Dexter's place was a shabby affair. Neither it nor the owner looked very prosperous, nor very clean. Dexter was short and paunchy, and he wore a dirty apron. It looked as though he hadn't pushed a broom around the room since he opened. He wouldn't meet another's eyes head on, and he had a whining note in his voice. Maybe the sum of all those traits was the reason his business was poor. At the moment, only one other customer was here.

"Bourbon, Cletus," Turner ordered. "Don't give us that stuff you palm off on most of your customers."

Dexter tried to look indignant and failed. He grinned slyly. "Would I try to fool you, Sam? The others don't know the difference. I'm not hurting them, am I?"

"You are, if they're paying for better stuff." Turner sipped at his glass. "It'll do," he grunted. He raised his glass to Jeff. "Here's to better days."

Dexter had a habit of butting in, even though the conversation wasn't directed at him. "There won't be," he said, "until every goddamned Mormon is run out of Missouri."

Turner glared at him. "That your thinking, Cletus? From the sound of it, I'd say Mace Nixon has been in here too much."

Dexter's voice rose angrily. "By God, he knows what he's talking about. I say put him in charge of things. He'd straighten them out in a hurry."

"Horseshit," Turner said contemptuously. "Too damned many of you thickheads are listening to him now. If you feel so strongly about him, why don't you join his company?"

Dexter couldn't meet Turner's eyes, but a defiant note remained in his voice. "I did. Last week."

"Oh hell," Turner said helplessly.

Red flowed up from Dexter's neck. "I guess you back the damned Mormons," he said aggressively. "Besides being petty thieves, they're immoral."

He bridled under Turner's pitying glance. "Don't try to tell me they're not. Ask Preacher Simmons what he thinks about them. You show me in the Bible where a man can marry as many women as he wants."

"Not wants," Turner corrected. "As many as he can take care of." He saw the lewd remark forming on Dexter's face and snapped, "Not the way you're thinking of. As many as he can support. I figure that's their business." He finished the rest of his drink and set the glass down on the bar with an angry thump.

"You had enough of this place, Jeff?"

Jeff grinned. "All I want." He set down his glass and turned to join Turner.

"You're no better than they are," Dexter shouted after them. "You'd like to be whoring around the way they are."

Turner didn't even dignify the remark by turning his head.

Jeff was grinning broadly by the time they got outside. "You're mellowing, Sam. Not too long ago you'd have been climbing over the bar after him."

Turner looked morosely at Jeff. "Maybe I finally learned that I can't whip everybody that's got a head full of nonsense." He spat as though he was trying to rid his mouth of a bad taste. "You should hear Preacher Simmons. He damns real good. If anybody does anything he doesn't approve of, he sends them straight to hell. Wouldn't things be in a sorry shape, if such men were really the right hands of God? Hell wouldn't be big enough to hold all the people they'd send down." He was silent a moment, then sighed. "Why do people get into the habit of listening to such speakers?"

"Maybe it's easier to listen to them than to think about what they're saying. Big mouths get more than their share of attention. Politicians learn that early. If they can talk loud enough, it doesn't make any difference whether or not they make sense, or tell the truth."

Turner chuckled wryly. "I guess I belong in that class. I did some fancy talking to get people to vote for me." The gloom returned to his face. "The way things are going now, I wouldn't get a dozen votes, if I ran again."

They were nearing Alverna's house. Jeff started to laugh at what Turner said, then cut it short. He peered ahead, swearing at the poor visibility of the night.

"What is it?" Turner asked.

"I swear I saw somebody slinking around the corner of Alverna's house. I caught just a glimpse of him."

Turner quickened his step. "Then we'd better go see who it is."

They turned the corner of the house and neither of them saw anything moving.

"Looks like I was seeing things," Jeff said.

"Maybe not," Turner grunted. "There's the shed. Too much livestock has been stolen lately. Both our horses are there. I'd sure hate to come out in the morning and find either of them gone because I was too lazy to look now."

He held up a cautioning hand as they neared the shed. "Horses seem pretty restless," he whispered.

Jeff heard the uneasy stamping of the two horses. It could mean something, or nothing at all.

Turner still wore his gun. Jeff was sorry he had left his in his room. "Yes," he said in a low voice. They split, approaching the shed's entrance from either side.

They listened again. That restless shifting of weight hadn't stopped; then Rowdy snorted.

Jeff nodded decisively. Something alien was in the shed. Rowdy never liked strangers. Jeff thought he heard a furtive step that had a different sound from the horses' stomping. He stabbed a forefinger at the shed.

Turner nodded. He had heard the step too. He motioned for Jeff to wait outside. Jeff decided that Turner's gesture meant the shed had only one entrance. He wanted Jeff to be ready to block somebody's escape, if he got by Turner.

Turner stepped into the shed with drawn gun in hand. "Who's in here?" he roared. "Don't make me shoot you."

"Hold it, mister," a frightened voice squealed. "I didn't mean no harm coming in here."

"Come out," Turner ordered. "And you be damned careful."

A slight, shaking figure came out of the shed ahead of Turner. The light wasn't good, but Jeff got the impression of a thoroughly frightened man.

"Who are you?" Turner demanded.

"North Mercer. I just wanted a place to hide tonight."

"Hiding," Turner jeered. "From what? You

were getting ready to steal a horse. We came back in time to catch you."

Mercer must have caught a gleam of light from Turner's star. "Are you a lawman?" Relief filled his voice at Turner's nod. "If you think I was going to steal something, lock me up."

"I'll do that," Turner said grimly.

None of this rang true to Jeff. It was abnormal for a person not to plead his innocence. This one seemed eager to go to jail.

"Wait a minute, Sam," he said. This was a thoroughly frightened man, running from something. He was full-bearded, stooped of shoulder, and hollow of chest.

"Who are you running from?" Jeff asked.

Mercer was shaking, and it was not caused entirely by the cold night air. "Mister, I came from Far West. It took me more than three days to work my way out of Caldwell County. You don't make good time when you're traveling on foot by night."

"You a Mormon?" Turner asked incredulously.

"I was." Mercer shook his head. "Not no more. I listened to Joseph Smith and thought he offered paradise to joiners. He's a damned liar. I found out it's a hell of a lot easier to join than to get out." Some of Mercer's self-confidence was beginning to return, for his voice became indignant. "I always thought you could join or leave a church, if it pleased you." He jerked his head in Far West's direction. "It sure ain't that way with that bunch."

Mercer's voice was firmer as he went on. "I thought when I got out of Caldwell I was all right. Just a couple of hours ago I found out how wrong I was." His tone picked up a tragic note of despair. "They're still after me."

"Who's after you?" Turner snapped. "And what for?"

"For refusing to obey my bishop's orders. He ordered me to marry Widow Grundy. She's in her fifties. The ugliest woman I ever saw. I can't bear looking at her. Doesn't a man have the right to pick the woman he wants to marry?"

Jeff shook his head incredulously. He didn't know what was going on in Far West, but if Mercer was telling the truth, and Jeff decided he was, he didn't like the sound of what he heard. That wasn't much above the slave level.

"Who's chasing you?" he asked quietly.

"Captain Fear Not," Mercer answered. The tremble had returned to his voice. "They give names like that to all the big officers in their army. Fear Not leads the Danites."

Jeff looked questioningly at Turner. Turner shook his head. He didn't know what the Danites were, either.

"The Danites are the avenging angels," Mercer explained. "If anybody does something the church doesn't like, the bishops set the Danites after them."

"Mercer, you talk too much for your own damned good."

The voice coming unexpectedly out of the darkness made Jeff and Turner jump. They had been so absorbed in what Mercer was saying that neither was aware that anybody was near them.

Jeff whirled and saw five indistinct figures. The men had crept up softly and were now close enough to have them pinned against the shed.

The one wearing a white overcoat was apparently the leader. He took another forward step. "You almost slipped by us, Mercer." He laughed with no mirth. He was tall and thin, and an aura of power surrounded him. He was bearded also. It was too dark for Jeff to make out his features plainly.

Mercer bleated in sheer terror, then moaned, "Captain Fear Not."

The captain laughed again, a low, hard burst of sound that grated on nerves. "Didn't you expect to see me again, Mercer? Wheeler thought he heard voices coming from back here when we passed the house. It's a good thing I decided we'd better take a look. You're going back to Far West to answer for your sins."

Mercer's trembling distorted his words. "I won't go." His voice rose shrilly. "The only sin I've done is that I want to quit your damned church." He threw out a pleading hand toward Jeff and Turner. "You've got to stop them from taking me."

"Shut your mouth," the captain said furiously. The other four surged forward at his motion.

"Stay back," Turner warned, his face turning savage. "I don't know what this is all about, but I'm going to find out. Who do you people think you are? You can't get away with this kind of stuff here. I'm the law in this town. All of you are under arrest until I get some more details."

He must have seen a new menace in one of them, for his hand darted to his gun butt. His hand never fully closed around it. Captain Fear Not was the closest to him. He lashed out savagely with his rifle barrel.

Jeff heard the dull, sodden sound of the barrel as it crushed Turner's hat down against his head.

"Why you bastard," he said in instant wrath. He never completed his step toward the captain. Somebody behind him hit him across the head. A brilliant display of lights burst before his eyes, then a sweeping blackness blotted them out.

CHAPTER 5

The pain held Jeff in its tenacious grip. He lay with his eyes closed, wondering why he felt so cold and damp. Why was his head pounding so? Against its onslaught he had to force himself to think.

Everything came back to him in a rush; the

threatening Mormons and Mercer. The one called Captain Fear Not had hit Turner, and another Mormon behind Jeff had knocked him out.

"Why, goddamn them," Jeff muttered. He opened his eyes and sat up. Both things were unwise, for they threatened to split his head open. He held his head in both hands, swearing dully as he waited for the vicious wave of pain to subside.

The waves died until he could think again. He had no idea how long he had been unconscious, but he had the feeling it was some time.

Turner lay on the ground a short distance away. Jeff crawled to him, fearing what he might find. That slash of the rifle barrel had been a brutal blow.

He blew out a sigh of relief as he saw and heard Turner's regular breathing. Probably Turner's hat had kept him from getting his skull broken.

"Sam," he said. He repeated the name several times before Turner opened his eyes.

Turner stared dazedly at him. "What happened?"

Jeff sketched the confrontation with the Mormons.

"Why, the slimy bastards," Turner said wrathfully. He made an effort to get to his feet before Jeff could stop him. The rush of pain changed Turner's mind. He sank back to the ground and put his head in his hands. At the moment, he could do nothing but swear at the pain.

When he finally raised his head, Jeff knew the

roaring ache was lessening. He had gone through the same experience.

"They got you too," Turner said dully.

Jeff nodded. "Before I could get to that captain, one of the others knocked me out."

"They took Mercer with them?"

"I guess they did, Sam."

"The poor bastard," Turner muttered.

"Yes," Jeff said shortly. "Feel like getting up?"

"I can try." Turner failed on his first attempt. He failed the second time too. He looked sheepishly up at Jeff. "Damned legs turned to spring," he complained. "Maybe you'd better give me a hand."

Jeff pulled him to his feet. Turner was wobbly, and Jeff gave him support. Turner was silent the first dozen steps toward the house. Jeff wondered if he hurt too bad to talk.

Turner's words dispelled that notion. "Jeff, the bastards aren't going to get away with it."

"We're not going to do anything about it tonight, Sam."

Turner started to flare, and Jeff said, "I don't know how long we were out. You can bet they got out of Gallatin as fast as they could."

"Then I'll ride to Far West in the morning," Turner said heatedly.

"We," Jeff corrected. "You thinking of raising a posse?"

Turner swore. "Damned if I'm not tempted to. I'd like to take in enough force to take that

Captain Fear Not out of Far West. But that could raise a hell of a stink. Maybe it would be smarter if we just looked around first."

Jeff blew out a relieved breath. He wanted to look Far West over, but he didn't want to light any fuses that he couldn't stamp out. Turner was mad, but not mad enough to quit thinking.

Jeff hesitated before he opened the door to the house. "Do you want to say anything about what happened?"

Turner scowled as he considered it. "I guess not. The fewer who know about it, the better off we'll be. It wouldn't take much to stir up an army to go howling after the damned Mormons. I guess I'm not ready to take that responsibility."

They stepped inside and headed for the stairs. Jeff hoped they would reach their rooms without encountering anybody.

Delight came into the hallway, dashing his hopes. Her eyes widened as she looked from one to the other, then lighted with a wicked spark.

"Sam, I'd say you pick bad company. He took you out and got you falling-down drunk."

Jeff's lips thinned. She was gifted with a ready tongue. He reconsidered that. The way she used it, if it was a gift, it came from the devil.

Turner showed his resentment. He hurt, and this was a poor moment to jeer at him.

"Delight," he said steadily, "you lacked one thing while you were growing up."

"What was that?" she asked incautiously.

"Alverna didn't tan your backside often enough."

Delight sucked in an outraged breath, then whirled and marched out of the hall.

Jeff shook his head in unconscious admiration. The angrier she was, the more regally she carried herself.

CHAPTER 6

Jeff led Rowdy out of the shed and mounted. "How are you feeling this morning, Sam?" Turner hadn't said a half-dozen words this morning.

"I've got a headache, and my hat doesn't fit too well. Otherwise I'm doing all right. How about you?"

Jeff's shrug showed a trace of irritation. He felt all right, though he wasn't in the best of moods. He had tried to talk to Delight this morning, and she stared straight through him.

"Delight bothering you?" Turner asked shrewdly.

"Enough," Jeff snapped. He had gotten off on the wrong foot with her, and maybe he would never recover that misstep. "Did she speak to you, Sam?"

Turner grinned sourly. "I don't see how she gets her nose so high in the air. That ain't her at all, Jeff. She inherited her ma's level head. Nixon's attentions have flattered her. She just hasn't seen through him yet. She'll get her eyes open before long."

"How far is it to Far West?" Jeff asked. He wasn't in the mood to talk any more about Delight. He didn't even want to think about her.

Turner shook his head in sympathy, but he was wise enough to change the subject. "Twenty miles," he answered Jeff's question. "Maybe more. Never measured it."

Both settled down for a long ride. They had gotten an early start, and the night had been cold enough to freeze the surface. It made for easier going, but that wouldn't last long. A watery sun was rising, and even its weak warmth would melt the thin coating of ice.

Turner broke the silence. "Alverna packed some sandwiches for us."

"Good," Jeff responded absently. Despite his effort, he couldn't stop thinking about Delight. She had reached him all right, and it left him morose and uncomfortable.

They rode quite a way before Turner said, "We just crossed into Caldwell County."

"Ah," Jeff said reflectively. He felt a tension creeping through him. This was ridiculous. Before Turner spoke, he hadn't felt that at all.

The countryside was empty, but Jeff kept glancing about him as he rode.

"You expect something to jump out of the brush at us," Turner jeered.

Jeff laughed mirthlessly. "Maybe I do. I know I feel tighter than when I started out."

"Me too," Turner confessed. "If that Captain Fear Not was any sample of the rest of the Mormons, we won't get much of a welcome."

"Did we expect one?" Jeff asked shortly. He would have to shape his attitude when he saw how the Mormons received them. "Sam, this must be pretty poor country."

"Why?"

Jeff pointed at a field. "Broom sedge." He indicated the thick growth of a knee-high brown plant. "A sure sign of poor soil."

"I wouldn't know about that, Jeff. But it figures. When Boggs split up Ray County he gave the poorer half to the Mormons."

Jeff stared reflectively at the broom sedge. This field was almost solid with the plant, and they had already passed many such fields. Whatever the Mormons got out of this land, they were going to earn.

Turner broke into his thoughts. "Shoal Creek's right ahead. We'll water there."

His jaw sagged as they came in view of Shoal Creek. "I'll be damned," he said in amazement. "I was through here several years ago. You couldn't see a single house. Now look at it."

Shoal Creek was lined almost solidly with the settlement. Jeff saw mills, shops, and stores, and everywhere people were busy at their tasks.

"They poured in here in a hurry, didn't they, Sam?"

Turner's face was sober with reflection. "My God, I had no idea this country was growing up like this. These Mormons sure settle a piece of land in a hurry." He looked at Jeff with concern. "Jeff, maybe the people of Daviess County got a right to worry. Maybe the Mormons will be thinking of taking up land outside of Caldwell County. With the way they're spreading out, it looks like they're going to need it."

"How can they get hold of it? The law says they can't buy outside of Caldwell, unless the vote is two thirds in their favor. That only leaves them force, doesn't it?"

"I don't know," Turner said uneasily. "After what happened last night, I'm about ready for anything. These people have grown so big that they're trying to make their own laws. If you cross them, you're in trouble." He glared about him at the people who were intently watching them. "Look at them. Doesn't it make your skin crawl? They must have an instinct for the presence of strangers, or else they sure spread the word around in a hurry."

Jeff nodded in sober agreement. Word of their arrival was spreading, for people hurried out of doors ahead of them to stand quietly and watch them pass. Several times, Jeff looked back. The people there hadn't moved. The impact of all those intent eyes had a peculiar weight that bore down on one's shoulders.

"Are we going to ask about our friend here, Sam?"

"I think we'll find him at Far West," Turner said. "It wouldn't do any good to ask. These people wouldn't give us the time of the day." He rode in brooding silence. "Jeff, I got the funny impression that at any minute, some of these people will stop us and say, 'You go no farther.' "

"I get the same feeling, Sam. What would you do, if it happened?"

Turner grinned sourly. "I'd say, yes sir. Anything you say, sir. I always was a coward when I had to face several dozen men alone. You know, I never gave a second thought to going anyplace I wanted to go in Missouri. I sure feel differently here."

Jeff nodded. He knew what Turner was trying to say. He had that interloper feeling himself.

They passed farm after farm, most of them small by Missouri standards, but all of them well cared for. From the looks of the harvested fields, Jeff would say that the crops had been good. He would be the first to admit that the Mormons had gotten everything they could possibly get out of this stingy land. In a half-dozen miles he hadn't seen a run-down place. These were hard-working, thrifty people. He thought with wry amusement, those are some of the traits that don't

59

endear them to their neighbors in Daviess County.

He pointed out another small group of people, who had come out of a farmhouse to watch them pass. "You couldn't get far in this country without being observed," he commented.

"Yes," Turner agreed. He looked half angry, half concerned. "Somebody's got them organized. It looks like a few people do their thinking for them. They're told what to do and how to do it. Maybe that system gets results, but it sure would stick in my throat."

"It's not the American system, Sam."

"It sure as hell ain't," Turner said fervently.

They climbed a small rise and stopped on its crest. A town was spread out before them.

"Far West," Turner announced.

Jeff whistled in surprise. He hadn't expected anything like this. At most, he would have thought that Far West would be a small, struggling town. This was a growing community, bursting at its seams with its own prosperity. It was several times larger than Gallatin. Jeff found it hard to believe that these people could accomplish so much in such a relatively short time.

Jeff judged the town site to be at least a square mile. It was laid out in blocks of over a hundred yards square. There were four principal streets, each wide enough for a dozen wagons abreast. Even the lesser streets were wide. Jeff thought of the older established Missouri towns with their narrow, crooked streets, starting out with no preconceived plans and winding aimlessly. The planners of Far West worked on a grandiose scale with a view to the future for growth. Every street ran at right angles to a large public square. Jeff saw signs of recent digging in the square. Whatever these people planned to build there was going to be big.

Turner looked at the town with a disgruntled expression. "I told you I'd seen it before. Damned if I thought it could grow so fast." He spit on the ground, the moody expression not leaving his face. "When it comes to planning, we could have borrowed some ideas from them."

Jeff pointed at a dozen men gathered at the outskirts of town. "Looks like we've got a welcoming committee."

"Don't see a hell of a lot of welcoming in them," Turner said grumpily, and lifted his reins.

They rode toward the waiting men. No expressions showed on those stolid faces. Perhaps it was their clothing and their beards that made them look as though they had come out of the same mold. Their rough clothing made them look square and stocky, and the low-crowned, wide-brimmed hats furthered the impression. Each was fully bearded, and the bulk of their shoulders and their hard, knotty hands attested to the hard work they had known.

"Howdy," Jeff said as he pulled up before them.

One of them nodded slightly. There was no other sign, no word of welcome. The one who nodded stepped forward and asked, "Why do you come to Far West?" He was a couple of inches taller than the others, and his manner said he had the authority to speak for them. His blue eyes had the cold sheen of a harsh winter day.

The question rankled Turner. "You ask everybody that who comes to your town? That attitude sure won't invite many people here."

That slight lifting of a lip might have denoted a wry amusement. "We're content that strange people do not come here."

Turner's jaw jutted forward. "Damnedest thing I ever heard of. How do you expect your town to grow?"

"It's grown faster than any nearby town you can point out."

That put a dull flush in Turner's face. "I'm the sheriff of Daviess County. Who am I talking to?"

Jeff watched with interest. It was likely that Turner wouldn't have his question answered. He had never seen more stiff-necked people.

The Mormon surprised Jeff by saying, "I'm Bishop Harmon. Now I must ask why you came here."

Turner crossed his hands on the horn and leaned forward. "I came here because some of your people broke the law in Gallatin last night. Five of them assaulted an officer of the law."

Harmon didn't even blink. "We don't consider we broke your laws. Captain Fear Not only carried out his duty. We consider you the offender. You interfered with that duty."

Turner's lips were a thin line, but he kept his control. "I want to see your Captain Fear Not."

Harmon considered that, then nodded. "You can lead your horses," he instructed.

Jeff dismounted, wondering if the bishop didn't like the idea of two gentiles riding while he walked.

Harmon led the way down one of the wide streets, the others of his group falling in behind Turner and Jeff.

Jeff tried to thaw some of Harmon's reserve. If the Mormons and gentiles were going to have to live together, some effort should be made to understand each other.

"Prosperous-looking town," he commented. He would guess that over three dozen houses had already been built. Most of them were log cabins, but a few frame houses had been completed, and a dozen others were under construction. He noticed two dry goods shops, three family grocery stores, and a half-dozen blacksmith shops. These Mormons must work a lot of metal.

Harmon didn't respond to Jeff's remark. Jeff felt his neck beginning to heat up. If this was typical of the Mormons, they were damned difficult people to know. He would make one more effort to break that flinty reserve.

"From what I saw of the farms, your people are good farmers. It gives a man a good feeling to see his land produce so well."

Harmon regarded him with speculative eyes. "The old selfish viewpoint. You claim sole ownership of everything you get your hands on, not realizing that the land is only loaned to you. No man here owns any land. All land is in the trustees' names, and forty acres is allotted to each farmer to work." He pointed out a huge, barnlike building just ahead of them.

"The Lord's storehouse. All crops are stored there and portioned out fairly."

For the first time, Jeff saw emotion in Harmon's face. His eyes were fired with a zealot's passion. "We have no needy nor lazy people here." He challenged Jeff's growing frown. "You don't approve of our way?"

Jeff wanted a few things clarified before he answered that question. "I suppose the farmer of that forty acres is told what to plant and how. Can he do anything on his own?"

Harmon's reserved manner returned. "So you don't approve?"

"Your way is not for me," Jeff said decisively. "It leaves a person no chance to make a decision on his own."

"You are blind," Harmon said with contempt. "But that will change too. You will see the light, or be destroyed. The Lord gave us this land with

His promise that He would make it bountiful. His promise came true as will His next one. The last message promises His people that they will own the whole world."

Turner could no longer remain still. "Bishop, sounds like you've got things mixed up. The state of Missouri allowed you to settle on this land. The state partitioned Ray County and—"

"Stop!" Harmon shouted. "You are lying. The Lord forced the state of Missouri to listen to His commands."

Temper flared in Turner's eyes, and Jeff said calmly, "Every man's got a right to his own belief."

Turner glanced belligerently at him, but he blew out a breath instead of speaking.

The party had reached the great, open square, and Jeff talked about it to quell heated tempers. This close, he could see how extensive the digging had been in the square. The open pit was some five feet deep and more than a hundred feet long. Its width was nearly equal to its length. Two cornerstones were already in place, great slabs of stone that had taken much animal and human muscle to move into place.

"Bishop, that's quite a hole," Jeff said. "What are you building?"

Harmon still had a pinched look about the mouth, and his answer was terse. "Our new temple."

"It's going to be quite an imposing structure."

Jeff sincerely meant that. "That trench must have taken a lot of days to dig."

"No," Harmon said flatly. "This was done in one day."

Jeff looked skeptically at him. He had noticed before that Harmon seized every chance to do a little bragging.

Harmon flared anew at Jeff's look of disbelief. "Five hundred men with mattocks and spades worked from sunup to sundown. Then we hauled the dirt away in wheelbarrows."

Turner still smarted from his last clash with Harmon. "How many men did you order out on this?"

Harmon's eyes were frozen. "They worked gladly. All our people work willingly for the Lord. But you couldn't understand that."

"I can understand one thing," Turner said flatly. "If you order everybody to work, it's not much different than slave labor."

Harmon flung up his head, and the zeal returned to his voice. "We do not believe in slave labor. Someday we will free the slaves in this state. Then we will release the world."

Turner sucked in a deep breath. "I know of nobody who owns slaves in Daviess County. But other Missourians do. No wonder you're getting so damned unpopular. You better learn to abide by the law."

"We follow the law the Lord gives us," Harmon

said passionately. "We do not follow laws that are wrong."

The two stared at each other, their mutual dislike naked and ugly.

Jeff thought uneasily, this disagreement between Turner and Harmon couldn't go much further without violence. If Harmon's temper burst its bounds, he could order them thrown out of Far West. Neither Jeff nor Turner could do a thing about it. Jeff could plainly see the wise course. Forget all about this Captain Fear Not and retreat with discretion. He knew how Turner would receive that suggestion. Turner had always been a firebrand, and this Mormon had tromped all over his toes. Jeff could appreciate how Turner felt, but this was a time when discretion was the better part of valor.

Harmon flung up a hand, and triumph flashed in his eyes. "Listen!" he commanded. "I thought it was almost time."

Jeff heard the faint throbbing of drums and the wailing of fifes. The sound grew in volume. Harmon had brought them here to see something specific.

A smug bragging was in the expressions on the Mormons' faces. It scraped Jeff's nerves raw. He held his gaze on Harmon until he forced Harmon to look away.

The beat of the drums was near them. Jeff looked back at the square. A company of mounted men trotted into the open expanse. Three companies of footmen followed, then another of horse, and still more came. Jeff's practiced military eye evaluated them. He would say between five and six hundred men were under arms. Too many of the guns they carried looked new, and the other weapons shone under the careful burnishing they had been given. His expression was black as he watched the companies march and wheel about the square. They obeyed the shouted commands of their officers with willingness and alacrity. There were no raw companies. They had been drilled long and well.

Jeff glanced back at Harmon. The fanatic zeal was washing his face again. Jeff saw everything as plainly as though he read it from a printed page. Information had been carried to Far West that two strangers were coming. Harmon and his group had waited for the strangers at the town's edge. They could have turned Turner and Jeff back there, but instead, Harmon had wanted the two gentiles to witness this display of strength.

The same thoughts must have been in Turner's mind, for he put them bluntly, "You threatening us?"

Harmon locked eyes with him. "Let's say I wanted you to see that we are capable of protecting ourselves."

Jeff looked at a new and far more menacing picture. Boggs had made some bad mistakes in dealing with these people. He had given them the right to raise and command their own militia. He hadn't been farsighted enough to see that that same militia could be readily turned against Missourians. Jeff softened his censure of the governor. Who could have foreseen that the Mormons were such a bold, aggressive people. They were Mormons first, last, and always. They had no concern for anything else.

A company marched past them, and Harmon said with wicked satisfaction, "Our Colonel Thunderbolt leads that company."

Turner and Jeff exchanged glances. Harmon correctly read the amusement behind those glances.

Harmon's face stiffened with resentment. "We name our officers for the qualities they possess. We have a Colonel the Intrepid and—"

Turner cut off the words by spitting on the ground at Harmon's feet.

Harmon's eyes blazed at the gesture of contempt. "One of these days, you will find our officers aptly named."

"I don't give a good goddamn what you want to call them," Turner said in rasping tones. "But you play your little games in your own back yard. I came to see your Captain Fear Not. I want to give him the same message."

Jeff studied the approaching officer. He hadn't gotten a close look at Turner's attacker last night, but he remembered that white overcoat. This officer also wore one. Jeff turned his head and said, "Sam, he's coming now."

"You can speak to Captain Fear Not when the drilling is over," Harmon snapped. "I advise you to use caution. He is not one to anger. He also leads our Danites."

Jeff and Turner watched the approaching captain. He looked tough and competent. He carried his lean, tall frame with a positive arrogance that dug into Jeff. He was fully bearded, the heavy shadow of his beard making the hollows in his cheeks more pronounced. From this distance, Jeff couldn't make out the exact shade of his eyes. He thought, somewhere near the color of slate, and let it go at that.

Turner spit again, coming nearer to Harmon's boot. Whenever Turner used that rasping tone, he was mad.

"I don't give a good goddamn what he leads. I'm going to teach him where to do it. It won't be in Daviess County again, or I'll throw his ass in jail so quick it'll make his head swim. That goes for everybody else who is crazy enough to follow him. When he gets out of Caldwell County, he's in another world with an entirely different set of laws. And by God, he's going to obey those laws."

Harmon's face was white with fury. He opened his mouth to speak, and Turner cut him short. "If you think those are just words, you try me and find out. Jeff, do you want to go and talk to Captain Fear Not?"

Jeff's grin was tight-lipped. "Wouldn't miss it for anything, Sam." He dropped Rowdy's reins and followed Turner out into the square.

Harmon yelled hoarsely at the two, but neither turned his head. They stepped in front of Captain Fear Not and blocked his passage. Jeff saw the startled flicker in his eyes, then they were unreadable. He was right about the shade, the color of slate on a cold, rainy day.

The captain pulled up short without giving a command to the ranks behind him. The front rank stopped without orders, and the others piled up against the first.

Jeff knew a sardonic amusement as he saw the fury ride the captain's face.

"What the hell do you think you're doing?" the Mormon yelled.

The company before Captain Fear Not wheeled on an order and hurried back. All military formation was lost, the orderly ranks changing into an ever-thickening ring, packing tightly about Jeff and Turner.

"I could have asked you the same question last night," Turner snapped. "I'm Sam Turner. I like to know who I'm talking to. And don't give me that game-playing name your bishop called you."

The Mormon's face reddened. For a moment,

Jeff thought he was going to refuse Turner's request; then he said coldly, "I am Stacey Trenton."

"All right, Trenton," Turner growled. He thrust his face close to Trenton's. "What did you do with North Mercer?"

Trenton's mouth partially opened, a silent inadvertent admission that he had confronted these two men last night. He had quick reflexes, for he recovered that impassive mask.

"Ah," he said. "That's hardly any of your business. Nothing would have happened to you two, if you hadn't insisted upon interfering."

Jeff had never seen Turner look angrier. Don't lose your head, Sam, he begged silently. With these numbers against us, they'd smother us before you take a half step.

Turner took a deep breath to steady his voice. "Maybe by your laws you think you had a right to do what you did. I'll grant you that much. But you can't ride into Daviess County and do anything you damned please. Do you understand that?"

They locked eyes. Trenton breathed harder than he had a moment ago. "What do you intend to do about it?" he asked.

Don't push it any further, Sam, Jeff pleaded silently. There's nothing we can do about it now.

Turner's breathing was uneven. "Nothing right now," he conceded. "But get this straight. If you ever ride into Daviess County again, you better be damned careful, because I'll be watching every move you make."

The onslaught was savage but controlled, momentarily leaving Trenton at a loss for words.

Turner spun on his boot heel and asked, "Coming, Jeff?"

Jeff was proud of him. Turner had handled a tough moment with dignity and decision.

Jeff felt a tightness between his shoulder blades as he walked away. The next seconds would depend upon what Trenton did. If he ordered an attack, Jeff and Turner would be run over.

"I give you the same warning," Trenton yelled after them.

Turner never slowed his step, nor turned his head. The ring before them slowly parted, grudgingly giving them enough room to pass.

They walked back to their horses and started to mount. Harmon stepped up to them, shaking with fury. This hadn't gone the way he expected.

"Don't you two ever come back to Far West," he said shrilly.

Turner swung up and looked down at him. "Right now I can't think of a single reason why I'd ever want to see this damned town again."

He rode slowly ahead, forcing Harmon to take a backward step.

Jeff felt an increased pride in Turner. Today's

events had increased Jeff's admiration. Turner displayed a maturity that surprised Jeff.

Jeff smiled to himself. If he ever voiced something like that, it would embarrass the hell out of Turner.

"I wonder what they did with Mercer," he mused.

Turner took it as censure and sprang instantly to his own defense. "What could I have done?" he asked half angrily. "I didn't even know where to begin looking for him."

"Don't you think I knew that?" Jeff replied. "I was sweating for fear you would do something that would touch them off. Poor devil. If he isn't dead already, he'll wish he was before long."

"They're so damned positive in everything they do," Turner growled. "It made me want to pound some sane thinking into their heads."

"The self-righteous always drive you crazy," Jeff said with wry humor.

The horses hadn't been shaken out of a slow walk, though Jeff felt an almost overwhelming longing to put as much distance as quickly as he could between himself and Far West. Without looking back, he knew all those eyes still stared at him. Their hostility had an actual physical impact.

"I had the funniest feeling back there, Sam."

"What was that?"

"I looked at Americans. I could understand every word they said. But I felt as though I was looking at foreigners in a foreign country."

Turner gave him a sober nod. "My feelings exactly, Jeff. What do we do about it?"

"It's past time to get a courier off to Aleck, Sam. Somebody has to get to Boggs and tell him what he's facing. I've never seen people more determined to have things their own way. Sam, I'm damned surprised that everything hasn't blown up in our faces before now."

CHAPTER 7

It was after dark when Jeff and Turner returned to Gallatin. As they approached the town, Jeff heard the beating of a drum and saw the flickering line of torches. His nerves jumped at the dull, heavy report of a small howitzer slamming back and forth between buildings.

He turned an unhappy face toward Turner. "If I didn't know where we were, I'd swear we lost our way and were winding up back at Far West."

Turner's expression was sour. "Without seeing them, I know what's going on. Nixon's damned Indians are meeting again. They do a lot of yelling, burn some gunpowder, get drunk, brag their heads off, and accomplish exactly nothing. He bought that damned howitzer for his company last month. They're a bunch of kids playing at being soldiers."

"Like the ones we saw in Far West, Sam?"

"Exactly," Turner snapped. "I swear there's not a brain in any of them. It scares the hell out of me to think what could happen, if both of them got heated up at once."

Jeff nodded thoughtfully. He contrasted the two leaders. From what he had seen of them, he would have to say Trenton was the more dangerous. "If I had to fight one of them, I'd rather it be Nixon."

Turner snorted. "Who wouldn't."

The howitzer boomed again. The bitterness grew more pronounced in Turner's voice. "All their yelling and shooting gets on my nerves. I wish to God they were doing something illegal. I'd like nothing better than to arrest the whole damned bunch of idiots." He lifted an eyebrow at Jeff's laugh. "What's so funny about that?"

"You wouldn't have enough room to put all of them away, Sam."

"That's the sad truth," Turner said gloomily.

Nixon's company was parading down Gallatin's main street as Jeff and Turner entered the town. Jeff winced at the contrast between this bunch and the militia he had seen in Far West. Nixon's Indians had no semblance of military order. They whooped as they cavorted and danced down the street. Every now and then they made mock threatening darts at the watching bystanders. They were in full Indian regalia, and a good percentage of them brandished tomahawks.

Delight stood on a street corner, the light from

the torches washing across her face. Jeff couldn't tell whether she was pleased or disgusted by the antics of the paraders.

Three of the Indians saw her and rushed toward her. Their painted faces and blood-curdling yells were enough to frighten anybody. One of them swished a tomahawk close to her head. Delight shrank back and squealed.

"Why, goddamn them!" Turner said, and started to spur toward the three men who were molesting Delight.

"Hold it, Sam. Let's see how far they go." He smiled wryly. "I've already learned she has a quick temper. If she explodes, maybe she'll look at Nixon with different eyes. They're his men."

"Ah," Turner said, in quick understanding. A satanic grin crossed his face. "You think quicker than I do, Jeff. Maybe your way will help to hang Nixon."

They sat back and watched the three pester Delight. Each time she tried to walk away, one of them blocked her path. They danced about her, screaming in her ear. Delight's boiling point wasn't very high. Jeff wished he could hear some of the imprecations she yelled at them. Her anger increased until she began striking out at them. They ducked and dodged, and her ineffectual blows set them off into peals of laughter.

"They're drunk," Turner said. "They could get rougher with her. Think we'd better stop them?"

"Not yet," Jeff replied. He wanted Delight so furious that her rage would include more than just these three. He hoped her rage would wash over Nixon because these men were in his company.

Turner's disgust was growing as he watched the antics of the drunks. "And Nixon brags about the protection his militia gives to the community. How would you like for your safety to depend on the likes of them. Makes you want to vomit, doesn't it?"

"It does," Jeff said curtly. Maybe he wasn't so clever in letting those three molest Delight. He guessed it was past time for him to swing down and knock hell out of them.

He started to dismount when he saw Nixon coming down the street. He resettled himself in the saddle. He was curious as to how Nixon would handle this. If Nixon was perceptive, he would get those drunks away from Delight in a hurry, then flood her with his apologies.

She didn't see Nixon coming; she was still engrossed with the drunks. She struck out at any of them that ventured close, she even kicked at one of them. She was almost sobbing with her rage when Nixon finally reached her.

Nixon touched her on the shoulder. She whirled, her hand rising. She recognized him before she struck at him. Her face seemed to collapse, and Jeff expected to see her tears flow.

Jeff was pleased with the way this was going. Nixon was taking the wrong approach. Instead of trying to appease her, Nixon was laughing, joining in the hilarity of the three offenders.

The rage was coming back to Delight, erasing the momentary weakness. She grabbed Nixon's arm with one hand, with the other pointing out each of the men who had tormented her.

Nixon lost a valuable chance to endear himself. Instead of listening to her with solicitous sympathy, he joined in even more with the drunks' merriment. Maybe he had been drinking too much himself, for he completely missed the shocked outrage that spread across Delight's face.

Jeff's eyes sparkled at the way this had turned out. Nixon was thickheaded, or he didn't know Delight very well. A wise person would have walked as though he was treading on thin ice when he first spotted her anger. Instead, Nixon joined the others and was laughing at her.

"He isn't very bright," Jeff commented.

"It took you pretty long to see that," Turner said.

Delight took a half step and tilted her head back until her lips were close to Nixon's face. Her move wasn't from any desire to get closer to him. She didn't want him to miss a word.

Jeff would have given anything to hear what she said. She looked like a raging she-cat whose tail had been stepped upon. Jeff would also have liked to see Nixon's face; he could safely bet that it was stunned.

She said what she wanted to in a few seconds, then spun on her heel and started away.

Whatever she said must have reached the three drunks too, for none of them tried to block her passage again.

Nixon was held dumbfounded before he sprang after her. He caught up with her and grabbed an arm. She whirled and struck the hand away. She must have had a few more choice remarks to make, for Nixon seemed to shrivel. She turned and strode away again. She carried her head high, and her shoulders were squared.

Turner whistled with pleasure. "You just saw a man cut his own throat."

Jeff hoped that Turner was right, but he was afraid of what would happen. Delight would simmer down, and Nixon would make his apologies. Delight would accept them, and the star-shine would return to her eyes. Maybe not, Jeff tried to reassure himself. Delight had a fiery spirit. It wouldn't take kindly to the dousing it had received.

Nixon said something to the three drunks and motioned out toward the street. They had a hangdog look about them as they moved quietly away.

"Nixon must have given them hell," Turner

observed. "He didn't care for them seeing Delight cut him down."

Jeff chuckled, thoroughly pleased with the way this incident had gone. Maybe this wouldn't completely change Delight's estimation of Nixon, but it would help.

"Sam, I've got to get a letter off tonight. Can you dig up a messenger? A thoroughly reliable man?"

"Tonight?" Turner asked with mild dismay. He groaned at Jeff's affirmative nod. "I was hoping you could put it off until tomorrow morning. Jude Harper's your man. But he sure won't be happy about riding out tonight."

"How much time have we got before this situation with the Mormons blows up in our faces, Sam?"

The question startled Turner. "How would I know that?"

"Exactly," Jeff said softly. "Maybe we'd better move while time is still with us."

Turner blew out a gusty breath. "I'll go find Harper. You writing Aleck?"

At Jeff's nod, Turner said, "Use my office. It's at the end of the block. I'll be back as soon as I find Jude."

Jeff turned Rowdy down the street. He winced under another blast from the howitzer. Maybe the spirits of Nixon and three of his people were dampened, but the rest of the Indians were still going strong.

He swung off before Turner's office. He placed an affectionate hand on Rowdy's withers. "You'll eat pretty quick."

He grimaced as he stepped into the office. Turner wasn't much of a housekeeper. He sat down and rummaged through the desk. He found a fresh piece of paper and a pencil. He wrote, "Dear Aleck," then paused and frowned into space, seeking a beginning point. The pencil started moving rapidly. He wrote that things were far worse than even Aleck could guess, that tempers were running hot and unpredictable. A few acts of violence had already taken place, and there were certain to be more. The cussedness of man was bursting out in a dozen places. It wouldn't take much more to turn this into open warfare. He described in detail what he had observed in Far West.

"These people were well-trained, Aleck," he wrote. "They're beginning to believe they're capable of whipping anybody who opposes them. Their weapons are plentiful and good. They believe they have the Lord's promise that all the land they want is theirs for the taking."

He paused and reflected upon what he had written, then started again. "Aleck," he wrote whimsically, "why does religion seem to bring out so much bad in a man? I know this; Boggs better move fast and call out the militia. He needs a big foot to stomp out this little brush fire before it gets into the timber. If it does, we've got pure hell on our hands."

He leaned back and reread what he had written. He could elaborate, but Aleck wouldn't need a lot of words to smell out potential danger. He imagined that Doniphan would take this analysis of the true situation straight to Boggs.

Jeff groaned as he thought of the time it would take for his letter to get to Liberty, Missouri, then for Doniphan to get to Jefferson City. It would take even longer to call out the militia and march it here. Jeff could only hope the situation wouldn't worsen too much before remedial measures could be applied.

He signed his letter just as Turner came in accompanied by a long, lanky individual. The newcomer had country written all over him, in his weather-beaten skin, in the huge, gnarled hands, even in his slight, permanent stoop.

"Jeff, meet Jude Harper."

Harper took Jeff's hand. Jeff thought he had big hands and a powerful grip, but Harper topped him. Harper had a shrewd eye and a taciturn mouth. Jeff didn't need Turner to vouch for Harper's trustworthiness. Jeff felt it instinctively like an invisible aura.

"Sit down, Jude," Jeff invited. "Did Sam tell you anything about what's bothering us?"

"A little." Harper had a country twang in his voice that matched the accompanying animal wariness. He would not commit himself until he was sure of his next step.

Briefly, Jeff sketched his impression as he watched the Mormon militia. "Jude, you could smell it. They're hunting trouble." He reflected upon that statement, then said, "Maybe that's a little unfair. But I wouldn't say they're avoiding provocation to set them off. I felt like I was smoking in a powder magazine."

Harper nodded soberly. "I was in Caldwell County a week ago. Didn't get very far. A dozen men stopped me and made it plain I wasn't welcome."

"Then you know what I'm trying to say." He looked at Turner. "Don't you keep a drink in this place?"

"On my salary?" But Turner pulled out a desk drawer as he spoke. He set the bottle and three glasses on the desk. He pulled out a handkerchief and polished the glasses. "Not very sanitary," he said, and grinned. "But this whisky is powerful enough to kill off the strongest germs."

He poured the three glasses and handed them around. Harper took his in a single swallow. Jeff foolishly followed suit without sipping at his whisky to test its potency. His eyes turned round and startled, as pure hell enveloped his mouth. For a moment, he was certain he would never draw another breath. Somebody had thrust a flaming brand into his mouth. He gasped, choked, and gagged, while moisture ran from his eyes.

It seemed forever before he could draw an unhampered breath and could talk.

He knuckled some of the water from his eyes and said indignantly, "Sam, that's the rottenest stuff I ever drank. I wouldn't give that to my worst enemy."

Turner had no feeling. He refilled Harper's and his own glass before he asked, "Jude, do you know what he's talking about?"

Harper shook his head. "Went down all right for me."

Jeff glared at them. Neither showed any distress after drinking the whisky. Jeff wouldn't touch another drink with a ten-foot pole.

"You've been drinking this kind of whisky too long," Jeff said. "It's burned out all your taste and feeling."

Turner grinned with relish. "I didn't tell you, Jude. He's an officer. They always were a weaker class."

A slow smile lighted Harper's face. "That's why they got so many enlisted men, Sam. To protect the officers."

Jeff broke into a laugh. Both of them were against him. It made for tough competition.

Harper brought the talk back to its former sobriety. "This Mormon militia any better than Nixon's bunch?"

"Nixon's bunch of clowns doesn't belong

in the same county," Jeff said with disgust.

Harper grinned with delight. "Nixon wouldn't be happy to hear you say that. His company's damned good. He told me that often enough. He never could understand why I wouldn't join him. If those Mormons are as ready to break out as you think they are, we'd better get something here that can stop them."

Jeff handed him the letter. "Do you know Aleck Doniphan?"

"I know him. Last I heard of him he was in Liberty."

"He still is. Jude, don't give this to anybody but him."

Harper's look was heated. Jeff didn't have to say that.

"You want this delivered as fast as possible?"

Jeff thought of the deadly purpose in the Mormon's drilling. He contrasted it against the drunken antics of Nixon's company.

"Just as fast as you can, Jude."

Harper waved away the proffered third drink. He gnawed off a chew and tucked it into the pocket of his cheek before he stood. "I'd better be getting on my way."

Jeff walked with him to the door. Harper was a good man. He saw what needed to be done and set about it without unnecessary talk.

Jeff and Turner watched Harper walk down the street.

"Quit fretting," Turner said. "Aleck will have that letter before tomorrow morning is out." He scowled as a drunken howl of laughter spilled out down the street. The laughter was followed by the heavy boom of the howitzer.

"Those sons-of-bitches will keep that up all night, if they aren't stopped." He hitched up his belt and stepped out into the mud. "I'm going to put a bug in Nixon's ear." He glanced back at Jeff. "You coming?"

"Wouldn't miss it for the world," Jeff said happily.

CHAPTER 8

Two men bent over the howitzer as Turner and Jeff approached. One was Billings, the other Dexter. Dexter was in his full Indian outfit. With that paunch he made a ridiculous-looking Indian.

Billings finished reloading the howitzer. "She's ready, Cletus. Touch her off."

Turner reached Billings just as he straightened. He kicked Billings with enough force to propel him forward in a series of staggering steps. Jeff didn't see how Billings retained his balance.

Billings whirled, his face wild. "Why, goddamn you!"

"That's for your smart-ass remarks last night," Turner said with open enjoyment. "I'm sick and tired of you shooting off that popgun. If you want to carry this farther, I'll be glad to oblige you."

Billings' belligerence oozed out of him. "You got no right to be kicking me," he blustered. "By God, Mace won't like it when he hears about this."

"Tell him," Turner snapped. "Here he comes now."

Billings whirled and looked down the street. Nixon, Owens, and Inman rode toward them. Jeff caught Turner's startled expression. Apparently, Turner had never seen these particular horses before.

These three animals were far out of the ordinary. Their ears were small and pointed. Their sleek look, their general nervousness, and those fragile, clean legs shouted thoroughbreds. Jeff was surprised that the animals weren't causing the riders more trouble. He wished Turner hadn't interrupted the shooting of the howitzer. Those thoroughbreds would surely have dumped their riders in the street.

He could appreciate these animals for their beauty and the purpose for which they were bred, but a thoroughbred would never be his choice. They could turn on a tremendous burst of speed, but they didn't have much endurance. Kentucky was filled with such animals, but it was surprising to run across them here.

"Mace," Billings bawled before Nixon reached

him. "Turner just kicked my ass. I wasn't doing a damned thing."

Nixon cursed Turner. He started to dismount, and the thoroughbred danced in little circles.

Nixon sawed on the reins until he could get the horse quieted. Jeff would say that Nixon hadn't been acquainted long with the horse.

Nixon finally swung down and handed the reins to Inman. "Hold him," he said furiously. He strode purposefully toward Turner, anger and whisky showing in his contorted face.

"Who in the hell do you think you—"

He got no farther. Turner met his approach by stepping into him and jabbing a stiff forefinger into Nixon's chest.

"Where did you get those horses, Mace? I never saw them before."

The unexpectedness of his attack made Nixon blink, leaving his face slack. "Why, uh—" he stuttered.

"Where did you steal them?" Turner demanded.

That question really jolted Nixon. He tried to cover up by yelling, "What do you mean steal?"

"You heard me." Turner stabbed the forefinger again into Nixon's chest. "I've never seen horses like that around Daviess County. I'm thinking you took them off of some Mormons."

Turner's guess hit home. Jeff could tell by the way Nixon's mouth sagged. It also stiffened his tongue, for he couldn't immediately find words to refute Turner's accusation.

"You rode into Caldwell County and took them, didn't you," Turner pounded at him.

Nixon's eyes were harried. He tried to throw back Turner's words, and his tongue wouldn't work.

"Don't try to tell me you bought them," Turner went on. "If you did, then you've got bills of sale."

Nixon's expression grew more flustered. Turner had him pinned against a wall, and he could see no way of slipping away.

"All right," he said in wild frustration. "We took them from two Mormons. We were only doing the job you're supposed to do. We came across them, leading these three horses. They ran when we yelled at them to stop. They left these horses, so we brought them in, hoping to find the real owner."

His expression wasn't so harried. Turner couldn't prove he was lying.

"You lying son-of-a-bitch." Turner's voice had a cutting edge. "Nobody in Daviess County has horses like these. I know it, and you know it. Did you steal these horses at gun point, or did you have to kill somebody to take them?"

Nixon looked at the ground. "Prove it," he said sullenly.

Turner's voice was brittle with anger. "I'm sick

of all this stealing. I don't care who does it. I'm going to stop it."

Nixon didn't lift his eyes. "What do you expect us to do? Take stealing from them without doing something about it? Me and my company won't stand for it."

The crowd, drawn by heated voices raised in anger, had grown steadily. Men yelled their approbation of Nixon's statement.

It strengthened Nixon's courage, for he could look at Turner. "We'll do the job you can't do. We'll stop all this stealing."

The crowd yelled louder.

"Hold it," Turner thundered, quieting the voices. "Get this straight. I won't have this raiding and stealing back and forth. I don't give a damn if it's done by Mormon or gentile. To me a thief is a thief. I don't care what kind of a tag he wears. Any of you lose any stock, you report it to me. Don't go doing anything about it on your own."

Somebody behind him hooted derisively.

Nixon's braggadocio was rapidly returning. "The people of Daviess can be thankful for my company of militia," he said pompously. "We'll protect them where the law fails."

"Don't give me any more of that horseshit," Turner said wearily. His tone showed that he knew he had lost the offensive. "Get this straight, Mace. Keep those horses close. If I find their rightful owner, I'm taking them away from you. Now clear this street. If I hear one more shot tonight, I'll arrest every damned one of you."

Turner swept the crowd with burning eyes, and sullen faces turned away. He turned and strode down the street.

Jeff stepped out to join him. The hooting rose again.

Turner didn't turn his head, though Jeff knew he was seething.

"Think you can find the rightful owners, Sam?"

"No chance. The Mormons won't broadcast their loss. You heard them say they'll administer their own laws. They'll also adjust their own losses to meet their idea of justice. They'll raid into Daviess and take whatever they think makes up their losses. Some poor devil will be hit some night when he doesn't even know the Mormons are near. He'll try to protect his stock and probably lose his life. If he lives, his hatred of Mormons will be a little more set. He'll burn to even up his loss."

Turner's shoulders slumped in defeat. "It's a goddamned snowball, Jeff. It'll grow bigger with every turn. How in the hell do you stop it?"

Jeff shook his head. There was only one answer to Turner's question. Force would have to be used, force so strong that nothing could stand against it. God, he prayed Boggs would act with dispatch and send out the Missouri Militia. If he didn't, Jeff knew Daviess and Caldwell counties were going to be thoroughly torn up.

"Well, losing sleep over it sure ain't going to do any good," Turner said as he opened the door to the Gibson house. "Wonder if we could talk Alverna out of a sandwich." He looked dubious. "Asking won't make her happy. She's got a set time for meals."

Jeff didn't blame Alverna. If she didn't keep definite hours, thoughtless people would keep her in the kitchen all night. But damn it, he hoped she would break her rule this time. His stomach screamed for food.

Alverna came into the entrance hall as they stepped into the house. She observed them with bright eyes. "You two look as though you're carrying the weight of the world on your shoulders."

Jeff sighed. "Close to it, Alverna." She was a perceptive woman. Although she could stubbornly resist somebody asking bluntly to be fed, if she saw how beat they were, she might offer food.

She cocked her head to one side. "Did you solve your problem?"

Jeff didn't shake his head at Turner, but Turner got his message and remained silent. Jeff could handle this.

Jeff smiled wearily at her. "Not even the smallest one, Alverna. When a day like this comes along, somebody crowds a dozen extra hours into it."

"Say," she exclaimed. "I'll bet you haven't eaten tonight."

"The last thing we ate today was those sandwiches you gave Sam this morning. I hate to think how far back that was."

"I wouldn't build a fire for the hungriest man in the world," she said decisively. "But I've got some cold roast left from supper. It will make good sandwiches. With cold milk, you'll get by."

"I wouldn't ask for anything better," Jeff said gratefully.

He sliced the day's fresh-baked bread while Alverna cut off thick slabs from the roast. Turner poured two big mugs of milk.

Alverna watched them tear into the sandwiches. After a few bites she laughed and said, "You look better. I never saw two unhappier people when you came in." She frowned in thought. "It seems that everybody who came in tonight was unhappy. Delight was furious when she came in."

Jeff grinned. "She had every right to be. Didn't she tell you why?"

Alverna shook her head.

"Some of Nixon's Indians were pestering her. They wouldn't let her pass. Instead of stopping them, Nixon made the stupid mistake of laughing at her."

Jeff chuckled at the memory. "From what I've seen he isn't the brightest person in the world."

None of them knew Delight was anywhere near until she spoke from the doorway of the kitchen. "So you just watched without making any effort to stop them." Delight's anger was all over her face.

Jeff looked as guilty as a hound caught sucking eggs. Then his face tightened, and his voice was crisp. "Why not. Why should I? I caught some of your tongue earlier this evening over Nixon. I couldn't see any percentage in risking more abuse."

Her eyes sparked, and red rushed over her face. "You don't believe in helping a lady when she needs it."

"Not when the lady doesn't know for sure herself," Jeff retorted.

She locked eyes with him, then turned and rushed away. Jeff was half angry, half sorrowful. "I guess I really tore things now, didn't I?"

Alverna was amused. "You don't know very much about women, do you? She'll be mad for a while until she does some thinking."

"Then she'll forgive Nixon," Jeff said gloomily.

Alverna laughed in sheer enjoyment. "I'd bet the other way. You gave her something to contrast against Nixon. If you had apologized, you would have weakened your position. Until tonight, I was worried about how she felt about Mace Nixon. Now I think there's every chance of that being changed."

Jeff's gloom didn't lessen. "I hope you know what you're talking about."

Alverna's laughter was a rich, rolling sound. "After this, you listen to me. I won't steer you wrong."

CHAPTER 9

Jeff was bone-tired with the accumulation of a week of exhaustive riding. Just the thought of moving made him wince. He could swear that he hadn't had over five hours' sleep any one night. It seemed that he no sooner shut his eyes when somebody rushed into town looking for Turner to report a new outrage. Jeff had insisted upon riding with Turner. Turner hadn't expressed his gratitude verbally, but it had been in his eyes.

Turner had the same haggard lines in his face. He stared bleakly ahead of him as they rode toward the Blanchard place. "The fourth raid this week, Jeff," he said. "Stock stolen on every one of them. But this is the first killing."

Jeff let his nod answer for him. Blanchard's fourteen-year-old son had ridden into town shortly after daylight. His pounding on the door had awakened Alverna, and she had aroused Jeff and Turner. "It's Steve Blanchard, Sam," she told Turner. "Something bad's happened to his father."

Steve Blanchard's words started out evenly

enough, but the leaking of tears betrayed him. He could no longer control his wild crying.

"Easy, son," Turner said, patting him on the shoulder. "Just take it slow and tell me what happened."

"It was the damned Mormons," Steve cried. "Pa heard something down at the barn and went out to see what it was. I was slow getting dressed. I hardly stepped out of the house when I heard the shot. I saw six of them driving away four of our cows. I didn't have nothing to stop them. Pa was dying when I reached him." The tears came anew, drowning out his voice. He buried his face in his hands, and his thin body shook convulsively.

Turner was beset by an anger he couldn't release while he waited for the crying to subside. "We'll be with you, Steve. Just as soon as we get saddled."

Steve knuckled his eyes. "I left Ma out there alone. She wants me to bring Preacher Simmons. I'll go tell him."

Jeff glanced at Turner's face as he rode beside him. Turner relived every moment of the earlier scene with the boy. Jeff could read the futility in his face. This trip out here would be no more productive than the rides on the other stock losses.

"You think it was the Mormons, Sam?" he asked.

Turner spat to his right. "I know it was. Even though Steve didn't catch more than a glimpse of them. I think the Mormons are paying back some of the losses they're suffering." He was silent a long moment, his face gloomy. "You can bet they're having losses too. We don't hear about them, because the Mormons don't think it'll do them any good to report them. They're taking care of their own. It's snowballing real good now."

He looked behind him. "Simmons got out in a hurry. Looks like he's collected a dozen men. You'll hear some hothead talk. Before very long somebody will be yelling that we should be taking out after them."

"You considering that, Sam?"

"I would, if it would do any good. But figure all the elapsed time taken up by driving those cows, the thieves have built up a good lead. They'll be deep into Caldwell County by now. If a bunch of armed men ride into that county, we set off a war. Oh, damn it. I wish I knew what Aleck is doing."

That makes two of us, Jeff thought.

The Blanchards, mother and son, stood by the body when Jeff and Turner arrived. Sarah Blanchard turned a beseeching face toward them. She showed the ravages of heavy weeping, but for the moment, she looked drained of more tears.

She spoke in a heavy, dull voice, twisting her hands as she talked. "The Mormons shot him down. Elmer didn't have a gun. He was a good man. He didn't have malice for anybody. All he asked was to be let alone."

Turner tried awkwardly to console her. "I know, Sarah. I don't know why these things happen."

Her eyes picked up a spark, turning her face fierce. "What are you going to do about it?"

Turner looked harassed. Jeff felt sorry for him. Turner had the kind of a job that caught hell from all sides. He was damned if he did and damned if he didn't. Luckily, Simmons and the others rode in, taking Sarah Blanchard's attention away from Turner.

Simmons was tall and lean, all awkward angles. He put a hand on her shoulder. "Terrible thing, Sister Blanchard," he clucked. "Terrible thing."

Preacher Simmons didn't impress Jeff at all. The skin on his throat hung in loose folds like a turkey's wattles, and his prominent Adam's apple bobbed with each word. He had bulging eyes in a nondescript face, and Jeff thought, nobody would pay him a second look if he hadn't chosen this profession.

Maybe his censure was too harsh, Jeff rebuked himself. Sarah Blanchard seemed to get solace out of Simmons' presence.

Simmons assumed authority, and men let him have it. Jeff was a little surprised that Turner showed no resentment.

Willing hands dug Blanchard's grave. Looking at Sarah's white, drawn face, Jeff thought, she can't cry any more. Simmons' funeral oration was too long, and Jeff was aware of feet shifting restlessly.

He was wrong about Sarah being unable to cry. The tears started again as the first clods were thrown into the grave.

Simmons stood with his arm about her shoulders. "This good man was killed by the godless Mormons," he said, his belligerent eyes sweeping from face to face. "Are we going to stand still and let this go unavenged?"

"No," they chorused back at him.

Jeff's ire rose steadily. Why were so many preachers, men of God, so militant? They punished with a heavy hand and promised vengeance with every other word. The Mormon's Bishop Harmon sounded much like this preacher. The words were the same, only the name was different.

Jeff knew he was asking for blame to be heaped on him, but he stepped in anyway. "Preacher, why do you call them godless men? From what I've seen, they seemed to worship the same God as we do."

Faces turned toward him, some of them angry, some stunned. Jeff didn't give a damn what they thought of him. He was sick of biased opinions. The more he saw of people as a mass, the more he doubted there was any basic honesty and truth left in them.

Simmons dropped his arm from Sarah's

shoulder and frowned at Jeff. "Are you a Mormon lover?"

"I am not," Jeff snapped. "But I think every man has a right to live as he believes. I also expect him to extend me the same privilege. I don't give a damn which side is doing the talking. I'd like to hear truth from both sides." He grinned bleakly at the outraged expression that molded Simmons' face. Besides tromping on Simmons' pet corn, he had practically called him a liar.

Simmons glanced about him to be sure he had the backing of the majority. "You saw what happened here. Can you deny that the Mormons are murderers and thieves? Everybody knows they are immoral. Do they observe God's sanctity of marriage? And you ask us to treat them kindly?"

Jeff groaned inwardly. This was an old, familiar argument. The plural marriages were the first thing thrown into any discussion of the difference between gentile and Mormon.

Simmons thought he had him on the run, for the volume of his voice increased. "Do you deny that they can marry as often as they want? I say they are immoral people, not fit to live around here."

Jeff's eyes smoldered at the murmur of approval that rose around Simmons. Simmons' face was getting that impassioned shine.

Simmons' voice rose. "They are murderers, thieves, and women despoilers, and yet you have the gall to try and tell me that they are God-fearing people."

Jeff swore at himself. He was a fool to try to reason with Simmons. Simmons could throw out impassioned, inflammatory words, but very few logical or reasonable ones.

"And you favor them?" Simmons sneered.

Jeff's face heated. "I never said such a damned thing. I said both sides had to be treated fairly. You don't think we've committed crimes against them?"

"No," Simmons said firmly. "We gave them homes and every consideration." He waved at the raw mound of the grave. "They repay it with this."

He drew a deep breath. "I'll tell you how they should be handled. Or better, I'll let Sarah tell you. She knows how to treat the Mormons."

Her face contorted with passion, and her voice grew shrill. "I'd treat them the same way they did my man. I'd kill every one of them."

Jeff knew he could not reach any of them, but he stumbled on. "Your husband was innocent of wrongdoing against them. Just as many of them are surely innocent of harming gentiles. Would you punish all of them?"

Her hating didn't abate. "All of them. Not a one of them deserves to be left alive."

Jeff thought he was going to be physically ill. How did God stand mankind? Maybe Jeff could find a small excuse for Sarah Blanchard, for she was under cruel stress. But there was no excuse for Simmons and his ilk.

Before he could speak, Turner roared, "All of you make me so sick I want to puke. Kill the women and children too. They're all Mormons." He faced Simmons, and Simmons quailed before the anger pouring out of him. "You call yourself a man of God. But you don't preach what He advocates. Why is it that a damned preacher can be so bloodthirsty?"

Simmons stared at him in shock. "Now just a minute," he spluttered.

Turner stared at him in disgust. "Come on, Jeff," he said, and started away.

"What are you doing?" Simmons bawled.

"You're as blind as you are stupid," Turner said. "We're going back to town." He never slowed his stride.

"You can't do that," Simmons hollered. "You're the law. You're in charge. You've got to catch the offenders and punish them."

Turner stopped and whirled. "You take charge. You've taken charge of everything else. You yell your head off for people to do as you say. Show them the way. But I'll give you a piece of sound advice. Don't go into Caldwell County after them. If you blunder over there, you'll never come back. Don't you know why? Because they've got about the same amount of humanity as you've just shown."

Jeff had never seen Turner angrier. He looked at Simmons before he fell into step with Turner. Simmons looked pale. Apparently, all the preacher wanted to do was to exhort men into action, then stand back and observe the results. Jeff doubted that Simmons would do any leading of these men.

"I'm showing my genius for making friends," Turner said sourly before he mounted.

Jeff just shrugged.

CHAPTER 10

Jeff sat across the dining room table from Turner. It was Sunday morning, and the house was quiet and empty. Alverna had left them a pot of coffee before she and Delight went to church.

Turner poured himself a cup of coffee and offered the pot to Jeff.

Jeff held up a protesting hand. "Hell no, Sam. I'm floating now."

"Good thing," Turner grunted. "I just about emptied the pot." This was supposed to be a peaceful day, but Turner didn't look as though he knew what day it was.

Four days had passed since Jeff's set-to with Simmons, and he hadn't ridden with Turner since.

"Any more reports of trouble, Sam?"

"Not from this side. But I think the Mormons would have every right to complain."

Jeff's eyebrows rose. "Why?"

"I passed Nobby Owens' place yesterday afternoon. He had a dozen head of as good-looking cattle as I've looked at in some time." Turner scowled into space.

"Go on," Jeff said impatiently.

"I wanted to know where he got them. He claims he bought them out of state. He's a damned liar. Nobby never had enough money to buy cattle like that."

"That can be checked out easily," Jeff said. "All you need is the name and location of the seller."

Turner looked at him in mock awe. "Now why didn't I think of that? When you've got enough time, I want you to teach me how to run my office."

Jeff laughed, his good humor undimmed. "You know what I'm saying."

"I know," Turner said gloomily. "You tell me what I'm going to do when Nobby forgot the name of the seller and has lost the bill of sale."

Jeff whistled softly. "He stole them sure as hell."

"That's a fact for sure, Jeff. But if nobody comes forward to report the loss, where do I go? My hands are tied until somebody comes around to tell me he's lost cattle."

Jeff drummed on the table with his fingertips. "You think he stole those cattle in Caldwell County?"

"I don't think. I know. With the help of Nixon

and his damned Indians, they made a raid into Mormon country. If those cattle had been stolen in Daviess, I'd have heard of it." He slammed the table with his fist, making the cups rattle in their saucers. "But where's my proof? The Mormons won't complain. But don't think they won't even up the score. They'll hit some poor devil who hasn't had any part in this trouble. If he tries to defend his property, he'll get his head blown off like Blanchard did."

His face was a tragic mask. "Jeff, it's getting ready to blow up in our faces. Can't you feel it?"

The tension had increased until Jeff could swear his skin crawled under the pressure. Captain Fear Not would be a busy man these days, taking out his Danites to avenge all the abuses the Mormons had suffered. Oh God, Jeff thought in frustration. Stacey Trenton and Mace Nixon were on opposite sides, but Jeff would never look at more similar men. They were both of willful dispositions, arrogant and thoughtless of others. They both carried flaming torches, eagerly seeking dry tinder into which to thrust them. If these two weren't stopped, Caldwell and Daviess counties would get a blood bath before they went up in smoke.

Turner asked a question that bothered him continually these days. "Jeff, do you think Aleck is doing anything about your letter?"

Jeff was sympathetic with Turner's concern. "You know he is, Sam. I don't know what's happened, but you can bet he's doing everything he can."

"Yes," Turner said miserably. "But day after day and we don't hear from anybody. It's like the rest of the world doesn't give a damn what's happening up here."

"It only looks like it," Jeff corrected. "It takes time to get a big body of men ready. Quit flogging yourself. You've done everything you could."

Turner breathed hard. "All I've accomplished is to lose what friends I had. I go down the street, and a lot of the people won't even look at me. The few who do have spit in their eyes. If there's much more of this, I'm going to mash some faces."

"If you want my help, Sam, I'm volunteering."

Turner fought to keep the grin off his face, then he laughed reluctantly. "I guess I'll wait, Jeff. Damn you, you always had a bit in my mouth."

They sat there, grinning at each other. This was a friendship tried by time and hardship, and each knew how much they could depend on the other.

Jeff heard the front door open. "Is that Alverna and Delight already? My God, we've wasted a lot of time sitting here."

Alverna and Delight came into the room. Delight's eyes were flashing, and her lips were a thin line.

Oh, oh, Jeff thought. Somebody, or something has crossed her.

"You should have gone to the service," Alverna said.

Jeff looked suspiciously at her. "You don't sound like you enjoyed it."

Alverna laughed ruefully. "Ask Delight about that."

Delight sat down, watching Jeff reflectively. She removed her hat and gloves.

Something was gnawing at her, and Jeff stirred uncomfortably. Things had been a little better between them ever since the night Nixon's Indians had molested her, but he still wasn't sure she approved of him.

"Will you tell me something?" she asked. "Honestly?"

Jeff smiled. "I used to think I was a pretty good liar, until I learned it wasn't getting me any place. I changed."

Those twin spots of anger were beginning to glow in her cheeks. "Don't make fun of me," she said with asperity.

He looked properly stricken. "I'm not, Delight. That's the furthest thing from my mind."

Those big, candid eyes studied him, and she was satisfied. "How bad are the Mormons?"

The question startled him, taking him completely off guard. He groped for a better understanding. "I don't know what you mean."

"What kind of people are they?" she asked impatiently.

He saw that she was struggling with some problem that she had to solve, and he picked his words with care.

"They're just people, Delight. No better, no worse than any others. They've got all the ugly traits other people have, and the same good ones. They've got a different religion, and like all other people they're blind when their religion is opposed." He sighed and shook his head.

Those lovely eyes rested on him a long moment. "Then you think both sides are about the same?"

"Yes," he said earnestly. "Tear the tag off of them, and you wouldn't be able to tell which is which."

"Then you don't think the Mormons are responsible for all this trouble?"

Jeff glanced at Alverna and Turner. They were listening with absorbed attention.

"They are not," he said promptly. "I wouldn't attempt to point out the one that started it. Sam put it well. He said we were watching a snowball growing bigger. One side turns it, then the other tries to outdo the first. It just keeps on growing."

Distress was beginning to show in her expression. "But they murdered Mr. Blanchard."

"They did," he said gravely. "And they've stolen stock. But how many of them have been killed, and how many of them have been robbed by us? That's the sorry trouble with people. Instead of trying to work out their differences, they only try to avenge themselves."

Delight still seemed reluctant to accept Jeff's explanation, but her defense against her people was weakening. "But how do you know?" she wailed.

"It's just a feeling, I guess, Delight. If something inside tells you you're wrong, then you'd better examine what's troubling you. What brought this on?"

Both her hands were tight, small fists. "Preacher Simmons' whole sermon was on the Mormons. I have never heard so much hatred and blood-thirstiness in anybody's words. Isn't it wrong for a preacher to talk like that?"

"It was pretty bad," Alverna interjected.

"I've talked to your Preacher Simmons," Jeff said. "Preachers are just people. They get mixed up just as easily as other people do."

"It was awful," Delight cried. "Mrs. Blanchard talked about her husband being killed. Then Preacher Simmons said that the Mormons had to be wiped out, man, woman, and child, until the last of the blight was gone. I've seen the Mormons. They look just like we do. They looked tired and cold and hungry. I tried to see them as the deadly enemy the preacher talked about, and I couldn't. But the others did. The room was filled with hate." She bit her lower lip. "That room wasn't a church at all."

Jeff regarded her with open approval. Delight had matured these last few days. Her youth could have stampeded her into going along with the majority, but she hadn't. She wouldn't accept another's thinking until she had examined it and learned whether or not it was acceptable.

"Mace made it worse," Delight said in a low voice. "He stood up and promised the people he would stomp out the last of the Mormons. They could depend on that."

"That's when we left," Alverna said. She looked at her daughter with sparkling eyes. "Delight couldn't stand listening to him any longer."

"This has to be stopped, doesn't it?" Delight asked. "It won't just die out by itself, will it?"

"It won't," Jeff responded. "I've sent for the Missouri Militia. It's going to take a force that big to stomp out such thinking and acting."

"From both sides?" she asked.

"Both sides," he said firmly.

A smile illuminated her face. "That makes me feel better. Sitting there listening to Simmons and Mace, I got scared."

"I can imagine," Jeff said. He felt a new rapport with this girl. They had discussed a serious problem and reached a mutual understanding. He thought of the old cliché, nothing ventured, nothing gained.

"Sam and I talked about the same thing while you were gone," he said. "I feel like my mind is packed with cobwebs. I'd like to get out into the air and blow them out."

"Me too," Delight said. Her lips were tremulous with unsounded laughter, and her eyes radiant. "Ma, may we take Betty and the buggy?"

By Alverna's small hesitation, Jeff doubted that Alverna readily loaned Delight her mare and buggy. Alverna wiped away his mounting fears of refusal by saying, "I don't see why not."

CHAPTER 11

Inman blew his nose. Damned if he didn't think he was coming down with a cold. He nearly froze in the church. Preacher Simmons was niggardly when it came to keeping the stove refueled. Inman had sat in the third row, and the heat hadn't reached him.

"You really had them listening to you, Mace," he said. They were a couple of miles from Nixon's home. Inman hoped Nixon would ask him in for Sunday dinner, but so far Nixon hadn't said anything about it. Nixon kept a hired couple, and the woman was a damned good cook. Inman had a cold stove in his house, and there wasn't much in his larder.

"Yes sir," he went on. "Nobby missed a good talk. You had them jumping up and down and yelling for you."

Nixon swelled visibly. "I did, didn't I?" He knew he could bend people to his will. He should be using that ability toward greater aims; he should go into politics. He had considered it off and on the past six months, and he nodded in sudden determination. He would run for public office, just as soon as he cleared out the infestation of Mormons in Missouri. The Mormons would melt and run just as soon as he turned the force of his company against them. The thought made his face glow with pleasure.

Inman didn't miss that pleased expression. He had better stay on the subject that brought that look to Nixon. "Nobby sure missed a good talk. I guess he stayed home to keep an eye on his new cattle." He couldn't keep the envy out of his voice. Damn it, why had Nixon given the cattle to Nobby. Nixon promised him the proceeds of the next raid, but Inman didn't know when that would be.

"Nobby's such a helpless little man," Nixon said. "I thought maybe I could get him started on the right path."

"Those cattle sure should start him right," Inman said. He didn't mention Nixon's promise to him. Nixon was a man of mercurial moods, and he couldn't be pushed.

Nixon laughed. "You think I've forgotten you, Hamp? Did you ever know me to forget a promise?"

Nixon frowned suddenly, and Inman said hastily, "I never did, Mace." He tried to plug the breach in Nixon's good humor. "I'm not squirming, Mace. I know you'll take care of me when the time is right."

Nixon's frown deepened, and his eyes picked up that intense glitter. Inman had seen Nixon work himself up into a rage before, and this was the way it had begun for no apparent reason.

"Mace, did I say something wrong?"

Nixon transferred that heavy frown to him. "You did, Hamp, when you said everybody yelled for me. Two didn't. Alverna and Delight walked out while I was talking."

Inman blew out a weak breath. Nixon's displeasure was none of his doing. "Aw, you know how women are, Mace. Maybe Alverna had something in the oven, and she had to rush home to take it out."

"It was more than that," Nixon said darkly. "I think that Karnes is poisoning Delight's mind. What's he hanging around here for anyway? I knew I should've taken care of him the first night I saw him."

Inman looked at Nixon's brooding face. He knew Nixon's next step. He would send somebody to run Karnes out of the county. Karnes would be a mean handful. Inman knew one thing for sure. Nixon wasn't going to order him to go after Karnes alone.

They rode around a bend in the road, and Nixon's head raised. He stopped his horse and stood in the stirrups as he studied the scene ahead of him.

"Somebody broken down, Hamp. Do you know them?"

Inman studied the wagon to one side of the road. It was a broken-down affair, and a sorry horse was in the shafts. The wagon had lost a wheel, and it was sharply tilted. A man and a woman stood at the wagon's rear. A third small figure sat in the wagon.

"Never saw them before, Mace." Inman's eyes widened at a thought. "Do you think they're Mormons trying to make their way into Caldwell County?"

"Very likely," Nixon snapped. "I don't trust strangers wandering around over our roads. They better be ready to give me some straight answers."

Nixon rode toward the wagon, and Inman lagged behind him. Nixon's eyes were narrowed and mean as he took a closer look at this outfit and family. The small figure on the seat was a boy perhaps five or six years old.

The wagon had seen too much hard service. The horse was nothing more than crowbait. The owner was stooped and frail. His cheeks were hollowed over a heavy beard, and he coughed before he spoke to the two horsemen. The woman, standing beside him, was heavy with child. She might have been pretty in earlier years, but now her weariness had drawn her face and wiped away any trace of beauty. She laid a hand on her husband's arm as though in fear, or in some sort of warning.

"I'm Enoch Dearborn," the stranger said. "And this is my wife, Melly. I thank God you came along." His eyes shifted before Nixon's merciless probing, and he licked his lips.

"My wheel came off," he continued. "I was fortunate enough to find the nut, but my jack is broken. I was unable to raise the wagon and put the wheel back on. I would be grateful to you for assistance."

Nixon stared at him with brutal directness, not acknowledging or returning the introduction.

"I only asked for help," he said in stiff affront.

"Where are you going?" Nixon demanded.

"To Haun's Mill. On Shoal Creek. My brother is there. We've traveled a long way to join him."

"That's a damned Mormon settlement," Nixon exploded.

Dearborn shrank back, recognizing the violence in Nixon. "We are Mormons," he acknowledged. "But we do nobody any harm."

Nixon swung down, his face alive with cruelty. "You must have come a long way not to know what's going on around here. All Mormons are liars, thieves, and murderers."

Fear mingled with resentment flickered in Dearborn's eyes. "You are wrong, my friend," he said stubbornly. "I don't know on what you base what you say, but—"

"Shut up," Nixon thundered. "I'll tell you what you are. You're a damned spy, sent out by your bishops. You want to find out where the best stock is so that you damned Mormons can steal them." Nixon's eyes were maniacal. "I've got a bellyful of Mormons. I'll give you something you can take back to your bishop." He swung and hit Dearborn full in the face.

Dearborn went over backward, the stunned surprise not having enough time to form fully in his eyes. His wife's scream was shrill and agonized.

Dearborn wasn't unconscious. He struggled feebly to rise, but his movements were uncoordinated, his eyes dazed.

"You lying bastard," Nixon roared. He stepped forward and drove a boot toe into Dearborn's ribs.

Dearborn groaned, his mouth sagging open under the onslaught of pain. Melly Dearborn screamed again.

Inman jumped to the ground as Nixon drew back his foot. His face was alive with cruel eagerness. "Save a part of him for me, Mace."

It was a raw day for a drive, but Jeff had tucked the lap robe around Delight as thoroughly as he dared. The mare's motion increased the wind's sharp bite. Ordinarily, he would have called himself crazy to go out on a day like this when there was no need. Being with Delight changed everything.

He stole covert glances at her as she drove. The wind had whipped high color into her cheeks, and her eyes were radiant. If she was enjoying this drive as much as he was, she wasn't even aware of the discomforts of the day.

He realized what had happened to him. His first admiration of her had deepened into something far more serious. A few times before in his life he had thought he was in love. Those times had been only a feeble imitation. This left him breathless and a little on the helpless side. It also left him elated and more alive than he had ever been.

He watched the movement of her gloved hands as she drove. She had strong wrists and competent hands. She wasn't driving a tired, plodding old mare. Betty was young and full of spirit, and it took constant vigilance to keep her from getting out of hand. If Jeff had a criticism of Delight's driving, it would be that she was on the reckless side.

"Jeff, did you ever find your first impression of someone completely wrong?"

Her question took him by surprise, and he took a moment to reflect over it. He laughed ruefully. "Most of the time."

She turned the full candle power of her eyes on him. "Why is that?"

She had to be talking about Mace Nixon. She was disillusioned with the man, and with her direct nature she wanted to know why.

"I don't know, Delight," he answered slowly. "Unless at first you see only the surface of a person. You have to know them longer to see deeper."

She chewed on her lower lip and frowned. "Maybe that's as good an explanation as I'll ever find."

Jeff watched her closely. He thought, She's feeling a sense of loss about Nixon, and she's trying to explain to herself the rapid switch in her feelings. He wisely didn't offer her any better explanation.

The bend ahead was a sharp one, and he was glad to see her slow as she approached it. She started to say something else, when a distant sound startled her.

"Jeff, that sounded like a woman's scream."

"It sure did." Jeff heard it again, higher and more anguished. "Somebody's in trouble."

He didn't have to tell Delight what to do. She lashed the mare with the whip. Going into the turn the buggy careened but stayed upright. Jeff gripped the handrail and hung on. He didn't censure Delight. That scream had sounded urgent.

He saw the wagon and horses first, then the small group of people standing over a figure on the ground. One of them was a woman. She struck ineffectively at the two male figures. A rough shove pushed her back, and she fell.

Jeff recognized the woman's attackers before Delight opened her mouth.

"Why, that's Mace and Hamp," she gasped.

"Yes," he agreed, knowing an odd anxiety. Her reaction would tell him a lot. If she tried to excuse Mace for what was happening, then Jeff would know she hadn't changed. He held his breath, praying that she would see only blame in what Mace was doing.

"Why, damn him," she said furiously. "What does he think he's doing?"

Jeff let out his breath, and suddenly everything was just fine. Everything Nixon did lately cost him more standing in her eyes. "We'd better go find out," he said.

Delight reached Nixon and Inman before either realized she was so near. Inman heard something first, for he whipped his head about. Jeff hit the ground running just as Delight fully stopped the mare.

Jeff tore into Inman, never welcoming a fight more. Inman was a slow thinker, for he didn't react well to Jeff's charge. Instead of retreating or trying to defend himself, he wasted a vital second or two trying to explain.

Jeff hit him in the mouth before Inman got more than a few words out. Jeff was sorry it was such a poorly aimed blow, for he wanted to knock Inman out. This blow was too high, mashing Inman's lips, instead of landing on the jaw. But it had enough force to send him staggering back-ward until his knees buckled, dumping him onto the ground.

Jeff whirled on Nixon. Nixon wasn't too fast a reactor, either. He had his hands up, but they were open; his palms toward Jeff. "Wait a minute," he said hurriedly. "You don't know what's going—"

"More than enough," Jeff snapped. He knocked aside one of the hands, leaving a clear path toward Nixon's jaw. Ah, that was a good blow. He could tell by the tingle that ran the length of his arm. Nixon reeled, his eyes rolling up into his head, leaving them blank and sightless. He hung there a moment, then came apart all at once. He fell into the road, slid a foot, and was still.

Jeff reflectively rubbed his knuckles. One of them was going to be sore in the morning. This was the way to end a violent argument, with one solid punch.

He turned, expecting to see Inman on his feet. But Inman hadn't gotten up off of the ground. He had a hand pressed to his mouth, and blood oozed between his fingers.

"What was that for?" His hand and the bleeding slurred his words.

Jeff grinned sardonically. "Only for beating a helpless man and knocking his woman around."

There was genuine amazement on Inman's face. "They're Mormons," he blurted out.

Jeff's face hardened. "That gives you the right to do anything you please to them?"

Delight rushed by him carrying the buggy whip, and her eyes blazed.

It took him several rapid steps to catch up with her. He wrapped his arms around her.

"Here now." That could have been a chuckle in his tone. "What do you think you're doing?"

"I could beat both of them senseless," she said passionately.

Now there was no doubt about the chuckle. He could have pointed out that one of them was already senseless, but he let it go.

"The woman they knocked down is carrying a baby," Delight said indignantly.

This was what a truly angry Delight looked like. Her nostrils pinched together with the rush of her breathing, her eyes poured out fire, and her bosom heaved. Jeff didn't let go of her. Jeff was glad her wrath was not directed at him.

"Go see to the woman," he coaxed. "She might need attention." At her hesitation he said softly, "Don't you think I can take care of them?"

She managed a rueful smile. "It looks like you can, Jeff." She turned toward the woman.

Nixon stirred and his eyes opened. He looked dazedly about him. He failed on his first attempt to sit up.

Jeff prodded him with a toe. "Get out of here, you miserable bastard."

Malice filled Nixon's eyes, and Jeff thought he was going to spit at him.

"You want another lesson?" he asked.

The resistance ebbed out of Nixon. He sat up and held his head in his hands. He tried not to make a sound, but Jeff heard his groan.

Jeff looked over at Inman. "Get him out of here. Right now," he barked. He took a step toward Inman. "I won't tell you again."

Inman scrambled to his feet at Jeff's approach. "We're going," he said sullenly.

Inman helped Nixon to his saddle. He was badly shaken up, for he slumped forward before he could recover. He gave Jeff a malevolent look and moved his animal.

Jeff thoughtfully watched them ride away. Maybe he was fortunate that this was Sunday and neither of them had carried a weapon to church. He suspected that both of them would give anything to look over a gun's sights at him.

He turned to give Delight assistance with the couple. The man had taken a beating, for he winced with each movement. He and his wife watched Jeff with fearful eyes.

Jeff thrust out a hand. "I'm Jeff Karnes. I can't tell you how sorry I am that this happened."

The fear began to leak away as the man timidly accepted Jeff's hand. "I'm Enoch Dearborn and this is my wife." His expression showed how bewildered he was. "Why did they do this to me?

I did no harm. I only asked for a little help."

"Either you told them, or they guessed you are Mormon," Jeff said gently. He felt pity for this man. His battering at Nixon's hands was evident. His general appearance showed how harshly life had dealt with him, leaving an indelible stamp of futility on him.

"It is not safe for a Mormon to travel on Daviess County roads," Jeff said. "The same holds true for gentiles in Caldwell."

Dearborn's bewilderment grew. "But why?"

Jeff held up his hands. "It's a madness, born of hatred from not knowing another, or even caring enough to try."

Dearborn licked his lips. "We carry no ill feeling for anybody. I was only trying to get to Haun's Mill."

Jeff had heard of the settlement, though he hadn't been there. "We'll escort you to the Caldwell County line. I can promise you, you won't be bothered again."

"I'll need the wheel put back on before I can move."

"We can do that. Delight, will you see what you can do for Mrs. Dearborn and the boy, while I help Mr. Dearborn."

Delight picked up the boy and held him close. Tears of fear were still on his cheeks, but he cuddled close to her. Mrs. Dearborn smiled timidly.

Jeff watched Delight with approval. She was a mixture of many things, and he found no fault with any of them. The boy was small, and very handsome. He certainly didn't get his good looks from his father. If Mrs. Dearborn once had beauty, it was overshadowed now by her recent terror and her advanced pregnancy.

"Let's see to that wheel," he said.

Dearborn pulled the nut from his pocket. "I was lucky enough to find it. But I couldn't raise the wagon and put the wheel on too. Melly wasn't able to help."

That was understandable. Jeff lined the wheel up next to the axle. After he lifted the wagon, he wanted Dearborn to put that wheel back on as fast as he could.

Jeff grunted as he put his back into raising the wagon. He had seen bigger and heavier wagons, but this one would tax him enough.

"Now," he said, and his breathing was strained.

Dearborn slid the wheel onto the axle. It seemed as though it took him ages to fumble the nut back into place. "Okay," he finally said.

Jeff's back and arms were beginning to scream their protest. He lowered the wagon and straightened, rolling his shoulders to ease the ache in them.

"I hope you've got a wrench," Jeff said. If Dearborn didn't have one, all this effort was wasted. Unless that nut was wrench-tightened, it would work off again before Dearborn drove very far.

"I've got one somewhere," Dearborn replied. He pawed through his possessions in the wagon bed, then his face lit. "Here it is."

Jeff tightened the nut, putting all his strength behind the wrench. Even then, he wouldn't guarantee that the nut would hold.

"Better check it every so often."

Dearborn nodded, and some of the dogged defeat left his face. "I'll do that. I don't know—" He searched for words that escaped him.

He was trying to say thanks, and maybe that was hard for him too. "Don't try to say it," Jeff said, and smiled.

He waited until the three Dearborns were on the wagon seat before he turned toward the buggy. He climbed up beside Delight.

She picked up the reins as the wagon moved off. "How long would Mace have continued to kick him?"

Jeff shrugged. Probably Nixon would have kept it up until he kicked the life out of Dearborn. He didn't want to tell her that.

"It wouldn't be hard for me to kill him right now," she said passionately.

He chuckled, and at her inquiring look said, "Just keep reminding me never to make you mad at me."

"They're just poor, ordinary people," she mused.

Futile was the word he would have used. Maybe that was one of the reasons Dearborn had joined the Mormon Church. He hoped to get the help he needed so badly.

The world was filled with such waifs. Jeff wanted to point out to Delight that she couldn't adopt all of them, but it was wiser to keep still.

"Oh, damn it," she said heatedly.

Delight was rebelling against the injustices in the world. She would tear herself apart and accomplish little.

"Things will be better for them when they reach their people." He tried to put more confidence into his voice than he actually felt. People like Dearborn lived out their lives in quiet frustration.

Her eyes were fixed broodingly on the rumbling wagon ahead. "Jeff, did you see that child? He had the face of an angel."

Jeff smiled. No boy would care much for that description.

"He has to grow up to something better," she cried.

He could agree to that, but then, that should be a grownup's wish for every kid.

"Yes," he said soberly.

CHAPTER 12

Jeff and Turner stood on a corner, watching Nixon and his company straggle out of town.

"Ain't that a brave display?" Turner jeered. "Make anybody cower, wouldn't it."

Jeff laughed. Turner was in a far better mood than last night. Yesterday, he and Turner had ridden out to check into another raid. This one involved more than stock stealing. Westhoff had been killed and his place burned to the ground. He was a bachelor, living only a few miles from the Caldwell County line. He lived well off the road, and the murder could have gone undetected for some time, if somebody hadn't seen a plume of smoke and investigated.

Nobody offered to ride out with Jeff and Turner. Outside of Alverna and Delight, he doubted that anybody in town looked with much favor on them.

They had followed the raiders' trail straight into Caldwell County. They had stopped and stared ahead for a long time. Turner shivered before he turned his mount. "Wouldn't do a damned bit of good to track them farther," he said.

"No," Jeff agreed.

"I got the feeling somebody's watching us right now."

"That could well be," Jeff said soberly.

Both of them had been wrapped in deep, black thoughts as they rode back to town.

They had talked about what was happening at length last night. Turner couldn't sit still. He paced back and forth in Jeff's room. "I've got to do something, Jeff. I looked at Westhoff's body, and I got fightin' mad. I'm about ready to cut loose and go after those damn Mormons. I can't stand much more of this."

"Everybody in town thinks you're protecting them," Jeff said quietly.

"Don't you think I know that?" Turner retorted. "I don't feel much sympathy for them any more. How many more dead men do you think I can stand to look at?"

Jeff didn't raise his voice. "You're only seeing one side, Sam. How much distress are the Mormons enduring? I told you about Nixon beating Dearborn. How much more of that do you think others of Nixon's kind are doing?"

Turner looked beaten. "I know you're right, Jeff. But we wait, and nothing happens. I'm getting damned disappointed in Aleck. I thought we'd hear something by now."

"We will." Jeff had to struggle to keep his tone positive. He too had expected to hear from Doniphan before now.

"I don't know what Aleck has run into," he went on. "But we'll hear from him. Tomorrow, or the next day."

He was a better prophet than he anticipated, for news had come in this morning. It wasn't from Doniphan, but it amounted to the same thing. General Atchinson wanted all the surrounding militia companies to come to Adam-on-Diamon."

"So they finally got off their ass," Turner said when he heard the news. "We're going up there, aren't we, Jeff?"

Jeff's face was alive. "Nothing could keep us away." Inwardly, he was still bothered. Why had Atchinson been selected to make the trip to Adam-on-Diamon. What was the practical purpose behind the meeting?

"We'd better get saddled up, Sam," he said as the last of Nixon's company passed. "It'll be near dark when we get there now."

Adam-on-Diamon was about ten miles from Gallatin. Jeff had heard disappointment expressed by Gallatin people that Adam-on-Diamon had been picked instead of them. Atchinson's choice was logical. Adam-on-Diamon was by far the larger of the two towns.

"I wouldn't be in too much of a hurry," Turner observed. "Didn't you see the way Nixon looked at you? He'll never forgive you for knocking him cold before Delight."

"So what?" Jeff asked impatiently.

"It won't be smart to catch up with his company on some lonely stretch of road. His men will take orders from him. Do you figure you and me can handle an entire company?"

Jeff grinned in wry amusement. "Might be a little difficult even with the kind he's collected."

They took their time, leaving Gallatin more than an hour after Nixon's company left town. Jeff cocked an eye at the gray, foreboding sky. He wouldn't be surprised if it snowed. It was the time of year when that could happen at any time.

He rode in silence, trying to guess at what Atchinson had in mind. It was an odd way to call out the militia. Atchinson had requested that the companies meet him in Adam-on-Diamon instead of ordering them to do so. The whole thing had a flavor of weakness, as though Atchinson was in a conciliatory frame of mind. If Jeff was guessing right, Atchinson wasn't going to accomplish a damned thing, unless he was determined to act forcefully on the Mormon problem. Jeff remembered too well the efficient militia he had seen in Far West, and the kind of men who led the Mormon companies. The first sign of weakness would embolden the Mormons.

Jeff shuddered involuntarily and Turner asked, "You that cold?"

"No," Jeff said slowly. "Somebody walked over my grave. Thinking the wrong things, Sam."

"I know how you feel," Turner said glumly. "I've got a bad feeling about this too."

Jeff noticed absently how black and cold the

water looked in the Grand River. In places it was frozen over, but the rapidly moving water kept it from freezing solidly.

Neither was in the mood to talk, though Turner did point out the old blockhouse on Splawn's Ridge. Jeff imagined it had been a valuable structure in the days when Indian danger was great. He sighed as he thought danger never seemed to abate entirely; it only changed its form.

The influx of militia packed Adam-on-Diamon's streets. Companies paraded up and down. Jeff didn't see two sets of uniforms alike. The captain of each company picked out uniforms that suited him. They ran the gamut of color and cut. The variety of choice was at distinct variance with usual military appearance. Nixon's Amaraguns stood out garishly because of their Indian dress and behavior. They whooped and danced in the street. The inevitable howitzer was dragged behind them.

Turner spat in disgust. "This is an army?" he said. "They look more like clubs out on a picnic. Scare hell out of you, don't they?"

Jeff grimaced. What he saw in the street was hardly a fighting force. They might do all right with a beer mug, but they sure wouldn't get anywhere going up against the disciplined Mormons he had seen in Far West.

The ordinary citizen of Adam-on-Diamon didn't have Jeff's doubts. The militia was here, and it was ready. Jeff heard individual after individual brag, "Now we'll see those Mormons run out of the country." Perhaps the words changed, but the meaning was the same. These people around here were as angry as the ones in Gallatin; they had suffered the same physical and material abuses. They were thoroughly aroused, and as angry blind as they were, they couldn't, or didn't want to see below the surface. Jeff heard too many recountings of stock losses, of burning, and killings. These people had every right to be steamed up, but what was marching up and down the streets wasn't going to solve their problems.

Jeff made a quick evaluation of the number of men in the militia companies. Somewhere around five hundred men, he estimated. That number wasn't going to be nearly enough to throw against the well-trained Mormon companies. His worry deepened and gnawed steadily at him. One pitched battle against the Mormons, and these ragtag companies would be running in wild retreat. He groaned silently. Damn Aleck. This wasn't the answer to the letter Jeff had written him. Jeff had spent great effort on that letter, going into careful detail of the situation in Daviess and Caldwell counties. If this sorry assembly was Aleck's answer to Jeff's letter, he hadn't read carefully what Jeff had written. His disappointment with Doniphan grew. Perhaps Aleck hoped that this small display of force would be enough to hold the Mormons in restraint.

It's not going to be nearly enough, Aleck, he thought. This wasn't the tactics of the Doniphan he knew. Doniphan believed, if a fight had to come, hit hard and first with decisive licks and not this pitiful fumbling Jeff was watching.

"Is Atchinson in town?" Turner asked.

"I heard he was," Jeff said gloomily. He wished he knew what Atchinson was going to do. Atchinson had military rank, but Jeff considered him more of a politician. If talk was needed, he might do very well, but Jeff was afraid the situation had gone far beyond the need of words.

"What do you think he's going to do with this militia?" Turner's eyes swept the street again.

"We'll find out soon enough," Jeff said. "The crowd is beginning to drift down to the platform."

He and Turner had seen the rough, makeshift platform at the end of the street.

The crowd thickened as it neared the platform. A stiff wind pushed the flames of the torches at each corner of the platform almost flat. Atchinson better have something worthwhile to say to this crowd. Jeff prayed that Atchinson wasn't here to whip this crowd into violent action. This force wasn't nearly large enough. Jeff had expected to see a statewide mustering. Damn it, Aleck, he said to himself. I said plain enough what was brewing here. He couldn't believe, with the facts that Aleck had, he would be so indecisive in action.

The men, gathered all around him, were in a mean, rebellious mood. The right word—he changed that to the wrong word—would send them roaring after the Mormons. If Atchinson did that, it would be the sorriest mistake he would ever make. Jeff shuddered as he thought of this rabble going up against the kind of men led by Captain Fear Not.

He tried to blot out such troublesome thoughts as he listened to the talk all around him. A man named Sellers reported nine horses stolen, and Johnson's barn had been burned.

"How long are we going to stand for this?" somebody yelled.

"No more!" The full-throated roar from the listeners had the animal-like quality of a pack of hounds, baying as they caught sight of their quarry. The only trouble was that the quarry these hounds were after was a long way from being at bay.

"They're getting it up here too," Jeff muttered in Turner's ear. "But I wonder how much thieving, how many killings are happening in Caldwell County?"

Turner showed his depression. "When a mess like this is stirred up, do you ever find out who started it, who is to blame?"

"Never," Jeff said decisively. "The only thing you can hope for is that it can be stopped without too much more bloodshed."

He cocked his head at the outbreak from the crowd. This had a new note, a savage eagerness. "Ah," he said. "Atchinson must be coming now."

Two men pushed their way through the crowd and climbed the few steps to the platform. One of them was Carswell, Adam-on-Diamon's mayor. Jeff knew Atchinson, though his contact with him had been infrequent. Atchinson was a stocky figure with intense eyes in a bearded face. He appeared to be self-confident, but agitation showed in the way his fingers played restlessly with the buttons on his jacket.

Carswell held up his hands to quiet the crowd. "General Atchinson brings news that all of us want to hear."

The crowd gave Atchinson a prolonged and ringing welcome.

"My God, they're treating him like he's the Savior coming to lead them to the promised land," Turner commented.

Jeff had a troubled insight. "Maybe they'll be disappointed."

Turner flashed him a piercing look. "What's eating you?"

Jeff didn't know. It was hard to give a vague feeling much credence. "Let's wait and see what Atchinson has to say."

"We're ready to follow you, General," a voice in the crowd yelled. "Let's run every Mormon back into Caldwell County. We'll teach them such a lesson they'll be afraid to stick their noses out again."

That brought on a new outburst of cheering.

Jeff watched Atchinson intently. Atchinson had a militant crowd on his hands. Men who weren't already in the militia would gladly join, if Atchinson said so. Jeff wasn't satisfied with the trend this was taking. This was a small local effort, and he thought it should be statewide. If Atchinson led this force into Caldwell County, it would only stir up additional trouble until an all-out war was the result.

Jeff thought the general looked too pale, or was it the flickering torchlight playing tricks on his vision. But Atchinson did keep picking at the buttons on his coat.

"I asked for this display of force to show the Mormons we mean business," Atchinson said huskily. "If their outrages against us don't stop, then—"

"Louder," voices in the rear interrupted him.

Jeff thought the ones near the platform were too stunned to speak. He felt that way himself. Atchinson wasn't proposing immediate action, he was merely trying to keep this crowd in check.

Anger was threaded through this new outburst, but now the anger was directed at the speaker.

Atchinson held up his hands until the clamor lessened enough for him to be heard.

"We have made a display of force. That will be enough to convince the Mormons that we are not fooling. Isn't that what we want?" An unconscious pleading was in his voice. "Nobody wants bloodshed if it can be prevented."

"I do," a voice yelled at him.

Other voices joined in, each shouting his personal accusation. "They stole my cows," one man yelled. "They've killed and burned. If you're not ready to stop them, then get out of our way."

Atchinson held up his hands, his face haggard. "You must not take independent action," he implored. "I promise you that Governor Boggs will—"

Derisive outcries washed away the remainder of his words.

Carswell waited until he could be heard. "Do you really believe that a display of force will change the Mormons?" he asked incredulously.

"I do." Atchinson tried to make the words firm, but they had a hollow ring.

"Then, General, you've wasted your time and ours," Carswell said contemptuously. "If this is your only solution, you'd better get out of the way and let us be at what we've got to do."

Atchinson's head flung up at the stinging criticism, then suddenly his resistance collapsed.

"I only tried to do what I thought best for all of us," he mumbled.

The crowd grew uglier with each passing second, and Jeff feared if they worked themselves up any more they could even do physical injury to the general.

Carswell felt the same way, for he said coldly, "I'll escort you back to your hotel, General."

Atchinson's shoulders drooped as he followed Carswell down the steps.

"We'd better give Carswell a hand, Sam," Jeff said in a low voice. "There's no telling what some hothead might do."

He and Turner stepped forward. "We'll go with you," Jeff said.

Carswell nodded. "It might be wise."

Atchinson glanced at Jeff. He knew him, but there was no recognition in his face. He had a crushing defeat on his mind.

Carswell forced a narrow lane through the crowd. Jeff and Turner flanked Atchinson. The general never looked up. That kept him from seeing the ugly looks flung his way, but he couldn't avoid the jeering words and curses hurled at him.

Jeff felt sweat breaking out on his forehead as they made their way through the crowd. In this mood, nobody could tell which way the crowd would turn.

Carswell escorted Atchinson into the small

lobby of the hotel. "You'll be safe now," he said icily.

Atchinson wanted to say something. He looked long at Carswell before he sighed and turned away. A beaten figure climbed the stairs.

"Why did he call a meeting in the first place?" Carswell asked Jeff. "My God, I thought he was sent here to furnish leadership."

"Evidently not," Jeff said. The lack of an answer to Carswell's question bothered him too. Atchinson hadn't accomplished a damned thing, except probably to hone tempers a little sharper. "What are you going to do now?"

Carswell helplessly flung up his hands. "I don't know. Who is the militia going to listen to now? There's a dozen different captains out there. They'll be fighting like a bunch of wild hogs over an acorn to see who comes up with the command."

Jeff winced as he thought of that rabble pouring into Mormon country. Crossing the county line was just about as close as they would get to Far West. "At the first threatening move, the Mormons would move in on them and cut them to shreds. That's not an army out there. That's a mob."

Carswell stared at him. "You're not exaggerating, are you?"

"Not in the least." Briefly, Jeff described what he had seen in Far West.

"They started it," Carswell protested. "They—"

Jeff cut him short with a savage slash of his hand. "It's too late to be fixing blame. Now, it's going to take an army, a real army to settle this. When you go back out there, you talk patience until a real army is put together. Convince them that until Boggs makes his move, they'll only be making things worse."

"That sure won't make me popular," Carswell said gloomily.

"It won't," Jeff agreed. "But you might save a lot of lives. What's Atchinson's room number?"

Carswell gave it to him. Jeff let his hand rest briefly on Carswell's shoulder. "Let's hope that they'll satisfy their warlike ideas by getting drunk. Maybe in the morning their heads will be too big to think of looking for trouble."

"I hope so." Carswell sighed and walked toward the door.

Jeff and Turner climbed the stairs and knocked on Atchinson's door.

Atchinson recognized Jeff after he opened the door, for he nodded stiffly. Resentment burned in his eyes. "I suppose you came to blame me like all the others."

"No, General," Jeff said. "But I am trying to find a sane answer to what happened out there."

Atchinson's brief flare of anger at Jeff's words faded, and he sank weakly into a chair. He didn't offer a chair to either Jeff or Turner. This was no friendly visit.

"Governor Boggs thought it would be an excellent idea to make a display of force to convince the Mormons that we meant business," Atchinson said in a dead voice. "He thought if someone with authority talked to the militia—"

"My God," Jeff broke in. His tone was incredulous. "You don't believe that did any good, do you?"

Atchinson wearily closed his eyes. Then he reopened them. "I guess not. I had no idea things had gotten so bad."

"Did you see Doniphan before you left Jefferson City?" Jeff asked.

"He has been talking steadily to the governor for the past week or longer. I do not know what he's been talking about."

"They better be talking about raising the state militia," Jeff said grimly. "If something isn't done immediately, Boggs has a full-blown war on his hands."

Atchinson's resentment stirred again. He didn't relish the thought that he had failed, that he was going to take a very unwelcome report back to the governor.

"Can't you understand what the governor is trying to do?" he asked. "He established the Mormon state in Missouri. He doesn't want to see his effort fail until he makes every effort to save it."

"Or is it that he hates to admit he is wrong?"

Jeff asked with brutal directness. "General, it's a common weakness."

Atchinson's temper was refueled, for the flash returned to his eyes.

Jeff forestalled whatever Atchinson wanted to say by pointing at him. "General, you tell Boggs he has probably made things far worse. Do you think the Mormons aren't aware of your meeting tonight? Do you think they're going to see strength in that mob out there? They'll see weakness. It may encourage them to make a bold attack, trying to stamp out their opposition. The Mormons are hurting too. They've suffered abuse and loss. I know from personal experience."

Atchinson tried to meet Jeff's challenging eyes and failed.

"I'll tell the governor what I've seen and heard."

Turner spoke up for the first time. "You better tell him to move damned fast. I sure as hell don't know how much time he has left."

He walked to the door, opened it, then stepped aside for Jeff to pass. Neither of them looked back at the man sitting forlornly in the middle of the room.

CHAPTER 13

A small brawl was in progress when Jeff and Turner stepped out onto the street.

Turner took a step toward the trouble.

Jeff yanked him back. "Let it go. You're not home."

Turner grinned sheepishly. "Forgot where I was."

A dozen drunks pummeled lustily, if ineffectively, at each other. By the variance in their uniforms, they were members of different companies.

"Probably an argument over who is going to boss who," Jeff said.

He heard a yell and looked toward the head of the street. Another fight was breaking out there.

"They'll be scrapping all over town before this is over," Jeff observed. "After tonight's failure, they're in a sore and quarrelsome mood. They've got to take their disappointment out on somebody. Maybe it's just as well. They may knock all the meanness out of each other. Let's get out of here before we're pulled into it."

"Suits me," Turner replied.

They got their horses and mounted. Jeff looked back. In the short interval of time before they hit the saddle, he could count three separate fights going on.

"If any Mormons see this, it's going to scare hell out of them," he said sardonically. "If the Mormons learn these fools are fighting each other, it might influence them to hit first and hard. In trying to hold the trouble down, Boggs may have torn the lid off."

"They can break their damned heads," Turner growled. He looked up into the dark sky, then rubbed a thumb across his cheek.

"I felt a snowflake, Jeff. That's all we need. A good snowstorm."

"You want to spend the night in town, Sam?"

Turner considered that, then shook his head. "We're all ready to leave. I'd just as soon push on. I'd rather be home in the morning than here."

By the time they reached Splawn's Ridge it was snowing hard. The snow was driven by the wind with enough force to sting their faces. Jeff remembered the old blockhouse they had passed on their way to Adam-on-Diamon. He couldn't see it now.

"Maybe we'd better hole up in the blockhouse until this lets up a little," he suggested.

"The last time I saw it, most of the roof was gone," Turner said doubtfully.

"The walls would shield us from the wind, wouldn't they?" Jeff argued.

"We could go see," Turner said.

They picked their way through a small grove of trees, taking it slowly for fear they would ride into one. They splashed through a creek wending its way at the foot of the hill. If Jeff remembered right, the blockhouse lay some hundred yards ahead.

He was beginning to fear they had missed it when the blockhouse loomed up before them.

Turner was right about the roof. Only one corner of it remained, but it was enough shelter for riders and horses to crowd under. It turned the snow from them, and the walls kept the wind from buffeting them. Both men swung off and walked about, stamping their feet to restore circulation in their numbed flesh. After a few moments the exercise and the body heat of the horses made it noticeably warmer.

"Almost cozy, isn't it?" Jeff asked, and grinned.

"Beats being out there in that," Turner agreed. "You want me to take the first watch?"

"Why? Do you expect somebody to follow us in this storm?"

"With everything as crazy as it is, I don't know who might happen along," Turner said stubbornly.

"You're right." Turner was spending his ounce of precaution wisely. "I'll take the first watch."

"You call me in a couple of hours." Turner curled up against a wall and was almost immediately asleep. Jeff listened to the soft, steady rumble of his snoring. Nothing kept Turner from sleeping.

Jeff moved occasionally to keep his circulation from getting too sluggish. He wasn't suffering too much, but he regretted they weren't spending the night in town. At least, he should have stuck a bottle in his pocket.

The snowstorm was hard but brief. He thought it was over in about two hours, but in that short time, he would guess almost two inches of snow were on the ground. The clouds split, and the moon appeared. Its hard, brilliant shine, with the snow as a reflector, picked up everything. Jeff could now make out individual trees in the grove.

His watch was up, but he delayed waking Turner. The snow blanket gave the earth a soft, ethereal beauty, hiding the dead leaves, the broken bits of twigs and branches, all the remains of last summer's living. It was too bad the snow couldn't do as effective a job on the mean ugliness in man's nature.

He started to waken Turner, then stiffened. At first, he thought that he was only hearing the wind, but the wind had died. He heard the sounds again, coming from the road, the soft thud of hoofs and snatches of voices without being able to hear the words. Then he saw a body of men moving along the road.

He didn't recognize the horsemen, but he felt no alarm. They would pass on by. He swore as he saw them turn into the grove of trees. It looked as though this band intended to spend the remainder of the night there.

The voices had more volume, and he heard occasional distinct words. One of the figures came into clearer view, and he stared incredulously at the feathers protruding from its head.

He wanted to laugh. This was one of the ironies of life. Nixon's bunch of Indians camped just below where he and Turner were.

He shook Turner awake, cautioning him to be quiet. "You won't believe this, Sam. Nixon just pulled into the grove."

Turner was instantly alert. "Is he coming up here?"

"I doubt it. The blockhouse would be too small for them. I think they'll spend the rest of the night where they are."

Turner moved to a wall and peered through a porthole. "Hey, it snowed quite a bit. They're going to have trouble starting a fire. It's Nixon all right. There's his howitzer."

Jeff moved to the next hole and peered through it. "They won't need a fire. Looks like they're loaded with bottles the way they're passing them around."

"I'd just as soon they stay where they are," Turner said. "I don't hanker to get into any arguments with any of them." His voice picked up a wistful note. "But damned if I wouldn't appreciate one of their bottles."

"I'll go down and get one of them for you," Jeff said.

He kept staring through the hole, and Turner asked, "What interests you so much?"

"I'm waiting until I see how Nixon sets up his camp." He swore in unbelieving tones. "My God, I can't believe it. He's not going to put out any sentries."

Turner shook his head. "And he calls himself a military man. Hell, he's camped too close to the road. Anybody passing by could be on him before he knows he has callers." He spat in disgust and shrugged. "It's his party. You'd better get some sleep, Jeff."

"Pretty soon." Jeff kept watching Nixon's camp. Somebody down there was ineffectually trying to light a fire. They were too drunk or didn't realize that the wood was wet. The laughter grew more boisterous. Another hour of drinking and all of them would be blind drunk. Jeff smiled sourly as he thought of Simmons' praise of Nixon and his company. He wished the preacher could see Nixon now. He waited a few moments longer. Nixon wasn't putting out sentries. He thought irritably, it's none of your business.

He walked over to the dry spot under cover of the roof. The horses stamped impatiently, and he could feel their body heat. Just the same he wished he had a couple of blankets, or a roaring fire to curl up beside. He pushed away that wish. He had slept cold before.

He had no idea of how long he had slept. He

came instantly awake and shivered. He pondered over what had awakened him. He decided the insidious, searching fingers of cold had been digging deeper into him, until he could no longer fight them off.

He stood and swore at the stiffness in his legs. He moved over to Turner.

"Everything all right, Sam?"

"Look at them, Jeff. They drank themselves into unconsciousness. It's almost dawn. Let's slip out of here." He colored at the criticism he thought he read in Jeff's face.

"Damn it, I'm not running away. Just looking at them makes me sick. If I talked to them, I'd likely start a fight."

Jeff smiled. He was in complete agreement with Turner. He looked out through a porthole. The blackness of the sky had weakened, turning to gray. The lighter streaks of dawn were in the eastern sky. It was going to be a clear day. The sun would rise shortly, though it might be weak and watery. Turner was right. There was no purpose in staying here longer.

"You let me sleep longer than you should have, Sam."

"I wasn't hurting, Jeff."

Jeff looked at the camp again. He wondered how long Nixon would sleep. That would be a sorry group of militiamen straggling back to Gallatin this morning.

He started to say something to Turner and stiffened. The poor light could be playing him tricks, but he was almost sure he saw shadows slipping through the trees.

"Sam," he called, the urgency pronounced in his voice.

"I see it," Turner said, his voice tight. "What do you think—"

Jeff cut him short. "I don't know." He didn't have the slightest idea who was making those skulking shadows. But that surreptitious approach boded no good for Nixon and his company.

"Get our rifles, Sam," he said.

He watched the shadows work closer to the sleeping men. He wished he had a stronger light.

He blinked to ease his straining eyes and felt the moisture in them. That wasn't imagination, either. A figure, in a white coat, led the other shadows. In another twenty, or thirty yards, those shadows would be able to stand over the sleeping men and pour a murderous fire into them.

Turner came back and slapped Jeff's rifle into his hand. "Ready to stop them?" he asked tensely.

Jeff squinted down the barrel and drew a long, slow breath. "Ready," he answered.

CHAPTER 14

Jeff picked out the figure in the white overcoat, but before he could squeeze the trigger, the leader slipped behind a tree. Jeff cursed under his breath.

Turner must have found his target, for he fired, then grunted, "That's one of the bastards."

Jeff didn't have time to comment. He was too busy trying to find his own mark. He fired. A figure straightened and whirled before it sank to the ground.

Turner was too occupied to talk any more. Jeff was aware that the figures, sleeping on the ground, were sitting up and staring bewilderedly about them. A few of them realized what was happening, for they put up a resistance quicker than their dazed companions. Another of the attackers dropped to the ground, and a fourth staggered.

The white-garbed figure stepped out from behind his protective tree and bawled, "The sword of the Lord and Gideon. Charge, Danites, charge."

Jeff discarded that ridiculous title, Captain Fear Not. He was dealing with Stacey Trenton and nobody else. He fired at Trenton just as he sprang forward, and cursed as he knew he missed. The damned Mormon had a guardian angel or was lucky.

He and Turner fired steadily, blasting holes in the attacking line that was working its way through the trees. The Mormons were paying a mounting price, and at the moment, Trenton probably did not realize where most of the punishing fire came from. More of Nixon's company were beginning to fight back, but their surprise had been so devastating that they showed only token resistance. Nixon was paying a price too. Men flattened out on the snow without ever getting to their feet. Jeff knew that until some order, physical and mental, came back to them, their defensive fire would be wild and too frantic.

Jeff got another shot at Trenton and thought he must have at least nicked him, for Trenton turned a startled face toward the blockhouse and jumped behind another tree.

"He knows we're up here, Sam."

Turner grunted. "He's got a creek to cross, then it's all uphill. He's going to have trouble getting at us behind these walls. Maybe Nixon will wake up enough to give us a little help." He squinted as he searched for another target. "Though God knows Mace doesn't deserve a chance to get even. Not after being caught the way he was."

Jeff fired again before he asked with wry humor, "Think Nixon will be grateful to us, if we do save him?"

Turner's chuckle had a mean note. "I can just see the bastard's happy face now."

Jeff ripped off a string of oaths as he missed another shot. He could blame his bad shooting on the poor light, though in all honesty he admitted that wasn't the real reason. He just wasn't shooting worth a damn this morning.

A long interval passed without another shot. "Think he's quitting, Jeff?"

Jeff doubted it. The little he had seen or heard of Trenton's actions he would say he was anything but a quitter.

He saw a massing of figures just inside the trees to the southwest corner of the blockhouse. Now Jeff could understand the quiet interlude. Trenton had pulled back and away to amass his attack on the blockhouse from a new direction. Jeff pointed the Mormons out to Turner and moved to another porthole to command this threatened sweep better.

"He could be taking a hell of a chance," Turner said as he joined Jeff. "It leaves Nixon behind him."

"Don't take Trenton for a damned fool," Jeff advised. "I'd say he's already sized up Nixon for the sloppy way he set up his camp. He has no fear of him. But he knows as long as he leaves us in this blockhouse, he's not going to be able to wipe out Nixon's company."

"You got him all figured out?" Turner jeered.

"I think so." Jeff's eyes gleamed. He felt the increased beat of excitement as he put his figuring against Trenton's thinking. He had no liking for this man, but that didn't dampen his respect for him.

"How does he know there's only two of us up here?" Turner asked suspiciously.

"He doesn't," Jeff said calmly. "But he could reason from the volume of firing from here that he doesn't have too much opposition."

"Then we'd better shoot real good," Turner said. "There's one thing I hate about it all."

Jeff peered through the porthole. "What's that?"

"I hate to fight without my breakfast."

Jeff chuckled, but he didn't look at Turner. The attack was beginning to form. The Mormons spread out and advanced on the creek, picking up speed as they neared the water until they were running at full speed.

"Hold it," Jeff cautioned. "Wait until they hit the middle of the creek." The water came up almost to the horses' knees. That depth would impede the Mormon charge. Jeff hoped his bad shooting was all out of his system.

At a time like this, a second stretched out into a minute and a minute into an hour. Maybe Atchinson had done some good with his aborted meeting last night. Jeff had credited him with the height of futility, but now he wasn't so sure. Atchinson said something about Boggs's hope that a display of force would check and put caution into the Mormons. It had done neither. Instead, the results were far worse than Boggs anticipated. Trenton had been in the neighborhood and had seen or been informed about the meeting. It had spurred Trenton into an open attack on Nixon's militia. Jeff could appreciate the move, for that was Aleck's belief; hit first and hard, not giving the enemy a chance to plant itself solidly. But this would backfire on Trenton. His action would force Boggs into taking counteraction. Now every militiaman in Missouri would be marching before this was over.

He stared down the rifle barrel. He was going to get Trenton this time. Trenton led the charge, and he was almost to the creek. He was yelling orders though Jeff couldn't make out the words. He would say one thing for Trenton; his men believed in him. They followed his orders with fervor and determination.

Jeff waited a second longer. Another step would carry Trenton to the middle of the creek. He centered the sights on Trenton's chest, said, "Now," and squeezed the trigger.

Trenton went down and under. Jeff had the uneasy feeling that something other than his bullet had knocked Trenton down.

He stared in outraged disbelief. Trenton's head reappeared, and he struggled to regain his feet. If Jeff had hit him, it didn't show. Jeff guessed that Trenton had stepped into a hole just a split-fraction before Jeff pulled the trigger.

An odd little tremor ran through Jeff. If he was

a superstitious man, he would say something out of the ordinary protected the Mormon captain. He shot at the moving, bobbing head and missed, seeing the splash of the bullet close to Trenton's head.

Other Mormons were reaching the bank closest to the blockhouse. Jeff better take his attention off Trenton and put some of it onto the Mormons before they charged up the hill.

He heard the hard slam of Turner's rifle. Turner knew what the top priority was, for he dropped a Mormon just stepping out of the creek. He shot again, and another went down, then crawled painfully away.

Jeff hated to take his eyes off Trenton, but he had better concentrate on breaking up this rush. He hit three shots in a row, and he didn't see a stir from any of the downed figures.

Only two defenders were in the blockhouse, but they had the advantage of height. The thrust of the Mormon charge wavered, and the hesitation grew more pronounced. The charge came to a full stop. The halt gave the Mormons time to evaluate what they were up against. The bodies, dotting the snow, the screams of the wounded were the last straw human flesh could bear. The ragged line took a backward step, then the backward step became a rout. Mormons ran madly to get away from those deadly guns.

Jeff fired once more, dropping a struggling

figure in midstream. He heard Turner's rifle report and felt in his pocket for another bullet. His fingers closed on a single shell, and he stared stupidly at it. My God, he was down to one shell.

"Sam, have you got any shells?"

Turner dug into his pocket. His hand came out holding four shells, and his face had the same stunned expression Jeff had had when he discovered how low he was on ammunition.

"Hell," Turner said in complete surprise. His pained attempt at a grin was more of a grimace. "If they try another charge, we won't be able to stop it."

Jeff nodded as he watched the fleeing Mormons. He searched for Trenton, but he couldn't find him. He was surprised that Trenton wasn't out trying to halt the wild retreat. Of course, Turner could have dropped Trenton without Jeff being aware of it. He looked from figure to figure on the snow. He didn't see Trenton, but that was still no proof. Trenton's white overcoat would blend in well against the snow.

The tension slowly oozed out of him. The Mormons had no intention of coming back. They had had more than they wanted. He heard a few shots from the direction of Nixon's camp and thought they were poorly aimed. Nixon could have made a move and thoroughly crushed the Mormons. Jeff suspected that Nixon had all the mauling he wanted too.

Turner had been doing some counting, for he said, "We dropped a dozen of them, Jeff."

Jeff shook his head. That was a pretty bad beating for a company to take. "We'd better go down and see how Nixon made out."

"Announce our coming loud and clear," Turner said. "I'll bet there's a lot of itchy trigger fingers down there."

Jeff couldn't argue with that.

They mounted and rode down the hill. Turner pointed at a wounded man, and Jeff shook his head, his jaw set. Those hit were Trenton's responsibility. He and Turner had wounded to look after.

He stood in his stirrups and hollered loud and long after he crossed the creek. Turner added his voice. Nixon's company was a suspicious bunch. They were well hidden behind trees, and none of them stepped out, or showed any part of themselves.

"God damn it, Nixon," Jeff roared. "Can't you see who we are?"

The long interval of silence was followed by a surly, "Come on in."

Jeff rode toward the figure that had stepped out from the trunk. Four bodies were on the ground. There should be more, though at the moment Jeff didn't see them.

"The dirty bastards," Nixon exploded as Jeff and Turner drew near. "They jumped us while we were sleeping. By God, if we'd been awake—"

Other men moved forward to crowd around Nixon. Each face had the hangdog expression of the beaten. Jeff looked at Inman and Owens. They didn't seem to be touched.

"You wouldn't have done any better," Jeff said in cold disdain.

"What do you mean?" Nixon blustered. "We stung them good. We forced them to run. What do you think those are?" He pointed at the forms lying near the creek.

Turner spat at Nixon's boot, forcing him to jerk it back hastily. "You didn't get any of them. You were too damned scared to even shoot straight." His wrath mounted. "You got what you deserved. Any damn fool that set up a camp like you did—" He was so angry he couldn't talk, and he paused to catch his breath. "You didn't have enough sense to put out guards. You begged for them to hit you. If Jeff hadn't seen them slipping up on you, every damned one of you would be dead."

Nixon spluttered in futile indignation, but Turner's words were getting through to Nixon's men. They looked uneasily at each other and scuffed up the snow with boot toes.

Jeff was enjoying this. Turner was ripping into Nixon good. He didn't need any help.

Nixon's gaze broke before the searing accusation of Turner's stare. "We could have taken care of ourselves," he said sullenly. "I was getting things organized when they turned on the blockhouse."

"Horseshit." Turner clamped his lips shut. The expletive said it better than anything else he could think of.

Jeff had been looking over the camp. He didn't see Nixon's prized howitzer. "Why didn't you use your cannon to beat them off?" The sarcasm in his voice was a cutting edge.

Nixon's lips were a thin, unhappy line. He had no intention of answering that question.

Inman didn't feel the same restraint. "The thieving bastards stole it. They—" He fell uneasily silent at Nixon's murderous glance.

Jeff wanted to roar with laughter. He had never seen a sicker-looking man than Nixon. He wondered if this fiasco knocked all the desire to play soldier out of Nixon. He held his mirth and asked, "Do you want help with your dead and wounded?"

Nixon looked at the ground. "We can take care of ourselves."

"Are you sure you don't want me to send wagons or help back from Gallatin?"

"God damn it," Nixon screamed. "I told you we'll take care of them."

Turner couldn't resist saying, "I hope you do better than you did before. Let me tell you something. Don't sit here on your ass too long. The

Mormons lost some men. They've got wounded. They'll probably be back to pick them up. If they see you still here, they might blame you for everything." That wicked grin was back on Turner's face. "Didn't Preacher Simmons call you the protectors of the people? I think he got you mixed up with a bunch of egg-sucking hounds."

The rage mounted in Nixon's face until it looked as though he would explode with it. Jeff tugged on Turner's arm and got him away from there.

They rode quite a way in silence. "The stupid bastard," Turner finally said.

"Yes, but do you think this changed him any, Sam?"

Turner pondered over that. "No," he finally said. "Nixon's kind never change."

CHAPTER 15

Missouri authorities were going to have to take a long, hard look at the interior of hell, for this morning's events had ripped off the lid. Turner had said something that Jeff thought fitted the situation well. Boggs had to get off his ass now. The time for recriminations and accusations was long gone. Now law and order had to be restored. That would mean the state's order, not the Mormons'. Would the Mormons fight, or submit. Jeff was positive they would fight. After what he had seen at dawn, how could he ever doubt the Mormons' fanatic determination. He shook his head in despair. Man was a stubborn, cussed animal.

"Jeff!"

The urgency in Turner's voice jerked Jeff's head toward him. Turner pointed ahead. The wavering plume of black smoke rose in the direction of Gallatin. Anxiety tightened Jeff's jaw muscles. The feeling worsened when he saw three more similar plumes. They all lay in a small, compact area. There was no doubt that Gallatin had been under recent attack.

Jeff spurred Rowdy into a hard run, and Turner pounded along behind him.

Maurer's house was the first one on the outskirts of town. The roof and walls had collapsed, and most of the wood had burned, though the charred embers still smoldered. Jeff reined up before it. The wind played with the column of smoke, distorting and shredding it. It also stirred the ashes, sending a dancing shower of them skyward.

He drove on for the heart of town. Three more houses had been fired. Turner called out the names of the owners. "Gilbrest, Summerskill, Hamilton." Like Maurer's house, nobody was near these three.

Turner scowled at Jeff. "Where the hell's everybody?"

Jeff couldn't answer that. This town gave him

an eerie feeling. He impatiently shook off that impression. Even four fires wouldn't have driven everybody out of town. He wondered if any attempt had been made to fight the fires. If so, the effort hadn't been effective.

Turner put Jeff's thoughts into words. "God damn it. Everybody didn't leave town, did they?"

"Maybe there's been an attack. Maybe the people are still hiding behind locked doors. If that's so, Sam—"

Turner hooted at the suggestion, breaking into Jeff's words. "Who could have attacked the whole town?"

"Maybe it was Trenton and his Danites," Jeff said quietly. It was a guess, unbolstered by facts, but it could have happened. If so, Trenton had had a busy night.

"What makes you so sure it was Trenton?"

"I'm not. But we know he was operating around here."

Turner kept picking at Jeff's reasoning. "Why would he jump an entire town? Hell, I can't believe—"

Jeff cut him short. "I wouldn't have said Trenton would jump Nixon's militia, but he did. Maybe he's taken all the pushing around he can stand. Damn it, don't you remember what Aleck used to say? If you're going all the way, make your move the first and hardest. Trenton did that."

A stunned expression was creeping across

Turner's face. "If you're right, Jeff, then it's started."

"Yes," Jeff said grimly. "I'd say Trenton fired these houses sometime around midnight, then moved on toward Adam-on-Diamon. He saw Nixon's camp and found another opportunity to strike. I'm guessing at how he figures. He'd hurt Gallatin and now he could stop any pursuit being organized to come after him."

Turner pursed his lips and scowled. By Jeff's reasoning, it all fit, but damn it, he would like to have something more solid than just guesses.

Jeff could see that the Gibson house still stood, but he wouldn't be satisfied until he saw Alverna and Delight were there and all right.

He turned and rode to the house. As he swung down, he had the feeling nobody was here either. He had experienced that feeling before. Whenever a house was empty, it had a lost lonely air about it.

He pounded on the door and called out several times. He frowned at the lack of response, and Turner said, "Try the door."

The door was unlocked, and Jeff stepped inside. He shouted Alverna's and Delight's names.

His frown deepened. Nobody was going to answer him here.

"I can't believe that everybody left town," Turner complained as they walked outside.

Jeff couldn't, either. But what if everybody had been driven out. The fear was a tight band, drawing closer around his heart until it became more difficult to breathe.

"We'll check every house and building, Sam." He wouldn't let the fear run away with him until he had searched the entire town.

The worry was beginning to gallop after he found six more houses empty. Turner looked at Jeff's hard, set face, and wisely did not speak. He could guess at the thoughts running through Jeff's mind. The people of a town couldn't simply disappear.

Jeff gripped Turner's arm, and his fingers bit in. "Sam, I just saw somebody look out of the church."

Turner blew out a breath of relief. "Then we'd better go see."

The church was a barren little one-room structure. As they approached, the volume of voices grew stronger. The harsh planes and angles of Jeff's face loosened. He should have guessed the solution before. The townspeople had gone to the church for the comfort of others' presence, and for the spiritual solace they might find there.

He stepped inside, and for a moment, he wasn't noticed. The people talked, but there was no life in their voices. From their listless attitudes, Jeff would say these people had taken a cruel, emotional beating.

His heart bounded as he saw Alverna and Delight. They were administering to wounded men in bloodstained bandages. Three bodies that would need no more attention lay on the floor.

"Delight," he said, trying to keep his voice from cracking.

She turned her head toward him, and her face went white and strained. "Jeff," she half screamed. She ran toward him, her arms spread wide.

His arms went around her, and he hugged her tight. He lifted and spun with her, giddy with relief.

She realized that every eye was on them, for her face flamed. "Jeff, put me down." She repeated it before he reluctantly complied.

He set her on her feet but still held her hands. He knew he beamed like an idiot, but he couldn't stop it. "I went to the house first," he babbled. "You weren't there. I died a little more at each empty house I found."

A soft tenderness was behind the radiance in her face. "I'm all right, Jeff."

It was a wondrous thing how much could be expressed without using many words. He thought he could kiss her and she would have been willing, but all those watching eyes restrained him.

His face sobered. "It was bad, wasn't it, Delight?"

His question brought her back to reality, and she gently disengaged her hands. "Bad enough, Jeff," she answered soberly. "Mr. Haimes, Davis, and Clayton were killed."

Three women cried in soft, broken sobs. Jeff

suspected that the hard, desperate weeping of the first brutal shock was spent.

"Mr. Lamont and Wilde were wounded," she continued. She shuddered at the memory. "For a while we were afraid they would kill everybody in town."

"The Mormons?" he asked.

His question to Delight unleashed most of the tongues in the room, and everybody tried to talk at once.

He held up his hand and patiently waited.

Preacher Simmons took charge. "It was the Mormons all right," he said shrilly. "May God strike all of them dead."

Jeff looked at him quizzically. "You're sure of that?"

"I'm sure," Simmons cried. "I heard one of them call the others avenging angels."

Turner and Jeff looked at each other, then slowly exchanged nods. Jeff's speculation was confirmed.

"But what started it?" Jeff persisted. There had to be something behind all this; it just couldn't break out of a clear sky.

"Nobody knows," Simmons said in a shaking voice. "They just rode into town and started shooting. Then they burned the houses."

Alverna came up beside Simmons. "That's not quite the way it happened, Preacher," she said quietly.

Simmons' face turned a mottled red and white. He tried to stare her down, but Alverna was a determined woman.

She smiled faintly as she looked back at Jeff. "I happened to be outdoors and saw everything that happened. There may have been fifty or sixty of them. They rode into town as though they were looking for somebody. They stopped Wilde and asked him where Clayton and Haimes were. He was trying to deny that he knew Haimes and Clayton when they came out of the saloon. They must have felt guilty, for they looked at the horsemen, then tried to run. They didn't have a chance."

"The Mormons just shot them down in cold blood?" Jeff asked incredulously.

"I thought so too for a moment," Alverna answered. "Then the leader raised his voice for everybody near to hear. 'This is a warning. These two men raided into Mormon land and killed and robbed. This is only a just repayment.' "

"Ah," Jeff murmured. He wanted a final confirmation as to who the leader was. "Did he wear a white overcoat?"

Alverna nodded. "He did. I think they would have left then, but Wilde ran into his house and got a gun. Lamont and Davis joined him, and all three fired. They hit one of the Mormons. I saw him sway in his saddle. The Mormons killed Davis and left Wilde and Lamont for dead."

Her face was strained as she related those bad moments. "They burned down four houses, Jeff, as a warning never to touch another Mormon."

She shuddered. "I thought they were going to burn down the whole town. I ran home as fast as I could, wanting to get Delight out of the house, in case they tried to burn it. But they left. All of us gathered in the church. None of us slept." She sighed, and the weary lines were etched deep in her face. "Nobody was sure they wouldn't return."

Jeff laid a reassuring hand on her shoulder.

Simmons opened his mouth again. "I wish Mace and his company had been here," he moaned. "Things would have been different then."

Jeff studied Simmons before he answered. "I'll tell you the only difference, Preacher. You'd have had more dead in the street, and they would have been Nixon's Indians. The same bunch of Mormons jumped Nixon in his camp. They hurt him bad."

He looked about at the shocked faces. He could have made the account far more difficult to hear; he could have told how Nixon had been stupidly caught and mauled. He wondered why he gave Nixon this little grace by withholding some of the truth. God knows he had no love for the man. Perhaps he was trying to save these listeners and not Nixon.

Shock deepened on Simmons' face, and he had trouble forming his words. "I don't believe it," he squealed. "The Mormons couldn't do that to Mace."

Turner had no desire to defend Nixon. "You don't think so, Preacher?" That mean tinge was back in his grin. "The next time you see Nixon, you ask him what happened to his howitzer. I'll tell you. The Mormons took it away from him."

Simmons sank down onto a pew and covered his face with his hands. "It is not true. It is not possible. God would protect Mace. He would defend him against the Mormons."

Jeff didn't blame Turner for wanting to smash this hardheaded man who couldn't, or wouldn't, see things as they were.

"It's an odd thing, Preacher," he said in a relentless voice, "how both sides scream at the top of their lungs that God only looks favorably on their side. That assumption gives them every right to commit any crime they want. I'd say that it's more likely that God isn't on either side. That both of them make him utterly weary of mankind."

He finished his tirade, and it was so quiet that he could hear people's breathing. None of them even tried to meet his eyes.

He turned toward Alverna and Delight and asked, "Ready to go home?"

Delight took Jeff's arm. "More than ready," she said, and walked out with him, her head held high.

Turner followed with Alverna. Outside, she called to Jeff, checking his progress. Her eyes danced with a quiet amusement. "After that call down, Jeff, I doubt if a single soul in town will speak to any of us again."

She cocked a speculative eye at him. "Was that true what you said about Mace being mauled by the Mormons?"

"Every word," Turner responded. "Me and Jeff sat up on a hill and had a bird's-eye view of the whole thing. Mace went to sleep without even putting out guards. As a military man, he's pretty good at parading but damned little else."

"Ah," Alverna said slowly. "No wonder you spoke with so much authority. Jeff, you and Sam drove them away?"

Jeff squirmed uncomfortably. He wasn't anxious to bring out his part. "We helped," he said, and let it go at that.

"Was Mace hurt?" Delight asked.

Was that concern in her face, was her breathing uneven? Jeff hoped not. But let danger threaten a person she once thought of with fondness, the resistance she had recently erected against him could be flattened.

"No," he said tonelessly. "He suffered some losses. He refused our help with his wounded."

"He is as thickheaded as ever, isn't he?" She sounded almost casual, but the familiar snap was back in her eyes.

He wanted to grab and hug her again, but that would have to be put off to another time.

Her face was grave. "Jeff, what will happen now?"

"Governor Boggs will have to call out the state militia. The Mormons have forced him into it."

"That means an all-out war," Alverna cried.

"That depends upon how determined the Mormons are. Yes, it could be very bad."

Alverna shivered. "I saw enough last night to do me for the rest of my life." Her eyes were shadowed with last night's memories. "Gallatin's too close to Caldwell County."

Jeff nodded. "Close enough. Stop thinking of Mace's company. You'll see a different militia. They won't be out playing games."

"Will Mace be called out too?" Delight asked.

"All the militia will be," Jeff answered.

"Then he'll get a chance to redeem himself," she said in a low voice.

"Or run," Turner said, and laughed.

Jeff thought her face clouded for a moment. Was she thinking of the Nixon she had known in better days? Did she want that chance for him to redeem himself? Did some of the better memories still have a tiny hold on her? He wondered in rueful jealousy if he would ever be sure enough of her so that not a shred of jealousy remained. He looked at her and thought, Probably not. Maybe it was for the best. It would keep him from ever being careless with her, or taking her affections for granted.

CHAPTER 16

Jeff beat a fist into a palm as he paced his room.

Turner lounged on Jeff's bed, watching Jeff with a judicious eye. "You keep that up, and Alverna is going to raise hell with you for wearing a path in her rug."

Jeff turned a worried face toward him. "Sam, when Jude returned from Liberty saying Doniphan had gone to Jefferson City, I sent Jude after him. That was eight days ago."

"A hundred and forty miles ain't no easy trip," Turner said.

"It shouldn't take Jude that long."

Turner tried to keep his worry from showing. "Ordinarily, it wouldn't. But this ain't the best time of the year to make a trip."

Jeff made another turn of the room. "I told him to get back as fast as he could."

"A lot of things could have happened—" Turner started.

"I know that, Sam." As troubled as the country was, several things could happen to a lone rider. He could be ambushed, he could have been disabled by a fall, or his horse could have gone lame. He jerked his thoughts from such thinking. That was borrowing trouble. A normal, sane reason could be behind Harper's delay. War machinery was a slow, ponderous thing. Getting it into motion took time and effort. Or Doniphan could have wanted Harper to remain. Jeff had to accept such a reason, or he would drive himself crazy.

"No trouble reported, Sam?"

Turner shook his head. "Maybe it's happening, but nobody's reporting it. I don't like it when it's this quiet." He grimaced. "I'm never satisfied. I complain when there's too much trouble and holler when there isn't any."

Jeff smiled sympathetically. Everybody in town felt the same strain. No matter what they talked about, their eyes pleaded, what's going to happen? Jeff wished to God he could give them some kind of an answer.

"Wilde died this morning," Turner said soberly. "He hung on tough, didn't he? I thought for a while he was going to make it."

"Yes," Jeff said wearily. "How did the towns-people take it?"

"Not as hard as I expected," Turner replied. "A little bit ago, they would have been hotheaded enough to grab for guns. They would have been screaming about going after the damned Mormons. The raid on Gallatin kinda beat them down."

"That's not hard to believe, Sam. What did it do to Nixon?"

Nixon had been in town a few times, but Jeff

175

hadn't seen him. Jeff was curious about Nixon's reaction to the beating he took.

Turner grinned. "He's cut way down. I haven't seen a single parade since he came back. Counting wounded and dead, I heard he lost seven men. I don't hear much talk around here about him being the people's protector. I did see something you might not like. Maybe I shouldn't tell you." He stared at his knuckles and popped them.

Jeff waited, then decided that Turner wasn't going to say anything more.

"Go ahead," he said impatiently.

Turner shook his head. "I never learned to keep my big mouth shut. Mace tried to talk to Delight last night. He stopped her on the street. It looked as though he didn't intend to let her by. I thought I was going to have to step out and read him out." He grinned wryly. "I should know Delight can take care of herself. I didn't see her say anything to him, but her eyes must have said plenty. He had that whipped-dog look when he stepped aside. She walked right by him with her head high. He kept up with her for a dozen steps, then gave up."

At Jeff's chuckle, Turner said, "Damned if I can figure you out. I thought you'd be madder than hell."

Jeff threw back his head and laughed. "I can't blame him for wanting to talk to her. If she wanted to talk to him, she would," Jeff said practically. "Nothing I could do would stop her."

"You afraid of her?" Turner asked with sly amusement.

Jeff started to deny it, then grinned sheepishly. Perhaps he was a little afraid of her, but not the way Turner meant. He would always be afraid of her. He would be a damned fool for not taking every precaution against losing her.

"A little," he admitted.

Before Turner could jeer at him, Jeff heard the knock on the door. He opened it, and Delight was there. That warm approval of him was in her expression.

"Somebody downstairs to see you, Jeff."

"Who is it?"

"He didn't say."

Jeff frowned. About the only people in this town who wanted to talk to him were in this house. But why were her eyes twinkling like that?

"He said for you to get downstairs right now."

His eyes widened, and a grin started at his lip corners and spread. He knew only one person who would give him an order like that.

He looked toward Turner. "Sam, Aleck's here. It has to be him."

He bounded down the stairs, Turner on his heels. Aleck Doniphan stood in the entranceway, talking to Alverna. "Aleck," Jeff yelled.

Doniphan turned slowly. He was an outsize man, standing six feet four inches, with shoulders to fit the height. He had dexterity in those huge hands, just as he had quickness in that big body. His mind was keen with the ability to pick out the parts that didn't fit the picture. He had legal training, and Jeff had seen him in action. He dominated the courtroom just as he dominated any other situation. He was in full uniform, and he hadn't picked up enough weight to make the uniform bulge or strain in any spot. He had thin, reddish hair, and even though it had been only a few weeks since Jeff had seen him, he thought Doniphan looked much older and very tired. He must have known some rough times recently.

"Aleck," he said again, and wrung the extended hand.

"Jeff," Doniphan said in that quiet, deep voice. The affection between the two men was evident in the prolonged handclasp.

Turner threw himself on Doniphan and hugged him. "Colonel, where in the hell have you been?"

Doniphan's booming laugh rang out. "Trying to straighten out the mess you made."

"Hell, Colonel," Turner said indignantly. "If you knew what's been going on up here, you wouldn't have daddled getting here."

"Sam, can't you see the stars on his shoulders?" Jeff asked. "You're not talking to a colonel any more."

Turner pulled back, a mock fawning on his face. "My God, a brigadier general. I forgot." He made a low bow. "If the general will forgive me—"

Doniphan looked at Jeff and shook his head. "Doesn't he have any respect for rank?"

"Never did," Jeff said. "But he's got a right to be upset. Where have you been?"

"Trying to butt heads with politicians," Doniphan said with a scowl. "Don't ever try it. The ordinary man doesn't have a thick enough skull to come out ahead."

Alverna took the opportunity to say, "Wouldn't you be more comfortable sitting down? I just took apple pies out of the oven, and the coffee is hot."

Doniphan smiled. "A hard saddle makes your first offer attractive. Poor scanty meals make your second offer irresistible."

Jeff led the way into the dining room and sat across the table from Doniphan. Turner sat on the other side of Jeff.

Alverna and Delight served pie and coffee and started to leave the room.

Doniphan stopped them. "Haven't you ladies any curiosity?"

"I have," Delight said with that gamin grin, and sat down.

Alverna seated herself with more dignity. "I didn't know whether or not it was proper."

"You'll hear no secrets here," Doniphan replied, a grim note in his voice. "All of Missouri surely knows what is happening, or will before much more time is out."

Jeff asked what was uppermost in his mind. "Did Boggs call out the militia?"

Doniphan washed down a bite of pie with a swallow of coffee. "Which one of you ladies made this pie?"

"I did," Delight replied. The faint wash of color betrayed her anxiety as to his judgment.

"I will never taste better," Doniphan declared. He looked sternly at Jeff, but his lip corners twitched. "You are a fool, if you ever let her get away from you."

The color deepened in Delight's cheeks. Jeff looked at her and said easily, "I've been thinking along that line. Aleck, will you tell us what's been going on?"

"I went straight to Jefferson City after I received your letter. Lucas kept me from seeing Boggs for a solid week." Doniphan's eyes darkened at the memory.

"Why?" Jeff demanded.

Doniphan made a savage slash of his hand. "The only reason I can see is that he wanted to keep reports of what was actually happening here from reaching the governor."

Jeff leaned forward. "But you finally saw Boggs?"

"I did. He refused to believe anything I told him." Doniphan smiled frostily. "He implied that a twisted man had relayed erroneous information to me."

"Oh, my God," Jeff said in open anguish. "What was his reasoning?"

"Pure hardheadedness, I believe," Doniphan said slowly. "Boggs formed Caldwell County against the advice of a lot of authorities. He hated to be proven wrong. Lucas was behind him all the way, backing him up."

Turner spoke for the first time. "Why?"

Doniphan pondered a moment before he answered. "I can only believe that Lucas wanted a brush fire to get out of control until it was a conflagration. Then he would command the militia that would have to be called out. Perhaps he saw how much credit he would get by whipping the Mormons." He shrugged. "Who knows what goes on in a politician's head?"

Alverna offered him a refill of coffee, and he accepted gratefully.

"After Jude reported to me with your letter, I got in to see Boggs again. I thought I was going to have to fight my way into his office. I found out how vindictive I can be. I enjoyed seeing his shock deepen as I elaborated on every detail Jude brought me. Lucas came in and strengthened my position. He told Boggs that the reports had steadily worsened in the last few days. He said he believed the Mormons intended building a foreign nation in the heart of Missouri; a nation with its own laws, its own army."

"He wasn't too far wrong in that," Jeff declared. "Boggs finally had to move?"

"He did. Somewhere near twenty-five hundred men are marching on Far West right now, Jeff. I sent Jude back to Liberty to notify my own brigade." He sighed heavily. "Once, I believed there could be no possible reason for carrying arms again." He stared bleakly at the far wall. "I am to meet the First Missourians just across the line in Caldwell County."

"When do we leave?" Jeff asked.

"As soon as I finish my pie. I'm glad you said that, Jeff. It kept me from ordering you to go." He looked at Turner. "Sam, you're going too. To the best of my knowledge, you two are the only gentiles who got into Far West. We'll need to know everything we can learn about their town."

Turner's face was awash with fierce pleasure. "You couldn't have kept me from going."

Delight's eyes were filled with anxiety. "It can be very dangerous, can't it?"

Doniphan let Jeff answer her question.

Jeff tried to soften his words. "It all depends on how determined the Mormons are. You heard Aleck say how many men are marching against them. Even the hotbloods among the Mormons will have to realize that their cause is hopeless against such odds." He smiled at her. "It's going to be all right."

He pushed back from the table. "I'll need a few

minutes to gather my stuff. I'll be down right away."

He packed his war bag and slipped into his heavy coat. God, how he hated a winter campaign. He wished the Mormons had waited until spring before they kicked over the traces.

He walked down the stairs, and Delight waited for him. Her face was pale, and she was strangely subdued. "The general and Sam said they would be waiting for you outside."

She had something to say, but it was sticking in her throat. Her eyes filled with tears.

"Jeff," she whispered. "You will be careful."

"The best I know how." Her face was tilted up to his, and tears sparkled in her eyes. "It means that much to you?"

"Oh, Jeff. I could not stand it, if—" She could not finish. Her arms rose and tightened about his neck. He bent his head, and his mouth closed fiercely on hers.

Who could say how long such a kiss lasted? It could have been only a fleeting second, or an eternity. Jeff only knew he was shaking when he raised his head.

"Aleck will court-martial me if I stay here much longer."

He gently thumbed away the overflowing tears. "With you waiting for me, nothing could keep me from coming back."

CHAPTER 17

"Ain't we leaving soon, Mace?" Inman asked. "The general was pretty impatient."

Nixon's face burned. That general had to give his orders to leave where Karnes was near enough to overhear.

"I don't give a damn what he said," Nixon snarled. He had tried to explain to Doniphan that his company had suffered grievous losses in his encounter with the Mormons.

"The loss of seven men isn't that serious." Doniphan's contempt had been naked in his voice. "You're under military orders now, Captain. Disobey them, and you'll be court-martialed."

Karnes had left with Doniphan then, but not until Nixon saw the mocking amusement on his face.

God damn him, Nixon raged. Everything had gone wrong since Karnes arrived in Gallatin. He had poisoned Delight's mind and turned her against him. Karnes had hit him when he wasn't looking and knocked him cold. Delight had seen that too. That damned Mormon, Enoch Dearborn, was the cause of a lot of his trouble. Nixon's embarrassment had worsened after the Mormon attack on his camp. His face turned vicious. He hadn't asked for Karnes's help. If Karnes had stayed out of it, he could have taken care of it by himself.

He ground his knuckles into the palm of his hand. God damn the Mormons. Nixon shifted his hatred to them. Doniphan's orders worried him. He didn't know how many militia companies had been ordered out, but there better be plenty. His one contact with a Mormon company was bitter in his mouth.

He would have to go or be stripped of all his military standing. The thought of that loss left him lonely and frustrated.

His eyes brightened. Haun's Mill was a small settlement inside the Caldwell County line. Missouri was at war with the Mormons. He could wipe out Haun's Mill and get personal satisfaction.

"Get ready to move out," he said.

"We're following the general?" Inman asked. He wished he knew what was running through Nixon's head. Those eyes had a hard, brilliant shine.

"We'll join him after we stop by Haun's Mill," Nixon said.

Inman's mouth gaped open. "What for?" That was in Mormon country. Inman hadn't forgotten the Mormon attack on them. He didn't want to run into any more of them. He wouldn't draw an easy breath until they joined the other Missouri companies.

"You questioning my orders?" Nixon demanded.

His burning eyes bored into Inman. "I can kick you out of the company and leave you here."

"Aw no," Inman said in quick protest. He had been nothing until he joined the company. He couldn't go back to that nothing. He licked a dry mouth. "You got me all wrong, Mace. Haven't I always been ready to do whatever you wanted?"

Jacob Haun had built his mill on the north bank of Shoal Creek. It was a small settlement of only twenty Mormon families, but it would grow. A half-dozen houses had already been built, but more were needed to take families out of tents and covered wagons. The blacksmith shop was almost finished, only the logs needing chinking to complete it.

Enoch Dearborn admitted it was pleasant living here, but a worry constantly picked at him. Since he had been here, he had heard not one quarrelsome word among the people. But they talked constantly of their fear of the gentiles. This was such a small world, surrounded by a hostile one. He thought often of the gentile who had gotten him out of that nasty situation on the road. The two gentiles who had attacked him had shown hatred of him because he was a Mormon. Why did there have to be so much hatred between peoples of different religions? He had tried to talk about such things with Haun, and Haun had jumped all over him.

"It is not us who hate," Haun thundered. "It is the gentiles. We only try to protect ourselves."

Dearborn had learned early not to question the things that troubled him so. He sat by the evening fires and listened to the others talk. Always the talk was the same; of the cursed gentiles.

Last night, he had heard a new and more frightening rumor. The Missouri Militia was supposed to be marching toward Far West. The unanswered questions again tormented Dearborn. Why did the Missouri Militia think it necessary to go against the Mormons? Would there be violence between the two religions?

He dared not ask those questions even of Melly. Melly was so close to her time. Would it be better for her to stay here, or should they try to make their way to Far West? He tormented himself by trying to decide which place would be safer.

He waited until the general talk broke up before he timidly asked Haun if he thought the mill was in danger of attack.

Haun gave his words frowning consideration. "No," he finally decided. "This is only a small place. The gentiles will pass it by. They will march on Far West and be beaten there. Do not fear, my friend. God is on our side."

Dearborn could not be as positive as Haun was. He could only hope that God had picked them and turned His back on the others. Obstinate questions flogged Dearborn's mind. Numerically, the Mormons here were weak and poorly armed. They had nothing but a few shotguns and squirrel guns. A solid band of timber and brush crawled almost to the north side of the mill. Gentiles could work their way through that thick cover and be upon the mill before anybody could sound a warning. He wanted to ask Haun, wouldn't it be wise to keep sentries posted, but he dared not.

Haun clapped him on the shoulder. "Keep your trust in God."

Dearborn nodded weakly and left him. He desperately needed somebody to trust, somebody to talk to. God was so far away. Because of her condition, he couldn't tell Melly of the worries that were driving him wild.

He spent a long and sleepless night. He guessed he was a man of little or no faith, for he could find no assurance regardless of which way he turned.

He was heavy-eyed and dragging in the morning. Melly had mentioned yesterday that today was laundry day, and he must help her in any way he could.

He tried to keep a bright face as he carried the soiled clothes to the wash house. He laid the fire under the large wash boiler and was preparing to go to the spring after buckets of water to fill the boiler.

The boy would trail at his heels every step of the way. Jed was a happy, obedient son, and

Dearborn's heart swelled with pride every time he looked at him. God had given him this son. Just looking at Jed should restore some of his faith.

He heard the shots, ugly and flat-sounding in the thick, morning air. They sounded as though they came from the thick stand of brush. His face went tragic as he heard the blood-curdling whoops and yells. It had happened, the thing he had so dreaded.

He picked up Jed, jerked off the lid of the boiler, and put Jed inside. "Stay there," he commanded. "Do not move until I come back for you."

He replaced the lid and ran toward the door. Melly caught him before he stepped outside. "Enoch, what is it?"

"Nothing," he lied. "You stay inside until I come back for you."

He ran outside, getting a confused impression of frenzied action with no seeming purpose. Men ran toward the blacksmith shop, some of them carrying guns. Dearborn looked at the timber north of the mill. He couldn't believe what he saw. Indians burst out of the timber, shooting and hollering at the top of their lungs as they ran.

This wasn't possible. To the best of his knowledge he had never heard of Indians being around here. A bullet slammed into his forehead, shattering all thoughts.

Melly saw him fall and ran screaming out of the door. She hadn't quite reached him when another bullet hit her. She hung upright for a long moment, a look of wonder on her face, then slowly sank to the ground.

Nixon's eyes glittered as he surveyed the scene. Men walked about the clearing, yawning and stretching before they settled down to their day's work.

"The damned fools," he muttered. "They haven't even put out any guards." That soothed his lacerated ego. Other people could make the same foolish mistake he had.

Owens and Inman lay beside him, the jerkiness of their breathing showing their poorly suppressed excitement. Other members of the company were crawling into place behind them.

Owens licked his lips. "What are you waiting for, Mace?"

A sense of triumph flooded Nixon. Nobody had seen them. "Nothing," he said, and aimed and fired. A man in the clearing fell as though his legs had been kicked from under him.

Nixon stood and waved his arm forward. "Come on, you Indians. This is getting-even time. Pay them back for killing your friends."

The company burst out of the woods, firing and yelling as they ran. Nixon stopped at the sight of a figure stepping out of a small building.

"That's him, Hamp," he called. "That Mormon we saw on the road."

He was filled with wicked satisfaction as he squinted down the barrel. This was the Mormon who had lost him Delight.

He squeezed the trigger. "Ah," he said as the figure slumped to the ground. "He won't give anybody else any more smart talk."

A second figure ran out of the small building, racing toward the body on the ground. Nixon fired again. The second figure collapsed as though every bone had melted.

"Hell," Owens said in distress. "That was a woman."

Nixon turned a savage face toward him. "She's a damned Mormon, isn't she?" He started running again.

Most of the Mormons broke for the large log building. A few ran across the mill dam to the south bank of the creek and found shelter in the woods that thickened just beyond the creek.

A few of the Indians wheeled to follow them.

"Let them go," Nixon roared. "We've got most of them in that building."

Nixon's company threw a ragged line around the blacksmith shop, each man crawling cautiously forward. They made individual forays toward the building, each darting on his own. When they stopped they poured another burst of shots against the walls.

The return fire from the building was sporadic and fading noticeably. Some of Nixon's Indians were now up against the walls, taking advantage of the wide openings between the logs, peering through them to locate their targets. The searching fire was brutally merciless. Now only an occasional shot came from the defenders.

"Break down the door," Nixon roared.

Some kind of a weak barricade before the door, was spilled aside by the charge of three men. They hit the door with their shoulders, and it flew open, almost catapulting them on their faces.

Nixon came in on their heels. A hail of bullets sprayed the interior of the building. In an instant, not a survivor was left.

A figure rose up from one corner, and Nixon fired at the indistinct object. He had the hazy impression that this figure was much shorter than the others.

He heard a high, shrill scream that kept rising higher and higher until it broke off on a note of despair.

Nixon advanced cautiously into the room. That last one he had hit looked dead, but he wasn't taking any chances on the well-known Mormon treachery exploding in his face.

Owens stopped beside him, both of them looking at the body. "My God, Mace," he exclaimed. "He's only a boy. He can't be over twelve years old."

Nixon stared at the white face frozen in a

grimace, and for a moment, a choking lump lodged in his throat.

He swallowed hard, and his face turned furious. "So what? Nits grow up to be lice, don't they? A couple more years, and he could be taking a pot shot at you."

Owens' face was empty. "Sure, Mace," he said weakly.

The slaughter in the blacksmith shop wasn't enough to satiate the bloodthirsty. Nixon's Indians prowled each house and poked into every tent, every wagon. Two well-spaced shots rang out. Inman grinned at Nixon. "Somebody found some life left in a couple of them."

"Yes," Nixon replied. He couldn't have wanted this to go off any better. He had smashed this settlement, and his company had suffered only two wounds. Childers had a shoulder wound; Bennet had a ball through the calf of his leg. Nixon would have to send them back to Gallatin, but he wasn't complaining about the cost. He had more than evened the score of his earlier defeat, and his self-esteem was restored.

He passed a small building and said, "Hamp, did you look in there?"

All over the compound, men were looting. They took what they wanted and complained about the poor pickings. Nixon grinned sourly as he listened to their bitter protests when they found very little worth taking. It was just as well. Nixon didn't want to join Doniphan with an assortment of booty.

"I'll look in it now, Mace." Inman walked into the building.

He came back out, shaking his head. "Nothing, Mace. Looks like somebody was getting ready to do a washing." His grin was evil. "The Mormons can't say we never did anything for them. We saved them the job of washing."

Nixon laughed and clapped him on the shoulder. He felt good, something he hadn't known for too long. After that embroilment with the Mormons at Splawn's Ridge, a hard ball of fear had lodged in his belly. That fear was gone now. Hell, hadn't he proven to everybody that the Mormons weren't so much?

Jed Dearborn was beginning to ache terribly. Curled up in that wash boiler, he couldn't move enough to relieve the creeping stiffness in his arms and legs. His mouth was parched, and his eyes kept filling with tears. At each shot he had to keep his mouth tightly shut to keep from screaming. His father wouldn't be pleased with him if he screamed. He wanted his mother. The tears welled afresh into his eyes.

It had been such a long time since he heard the last shot. Surely, he could get out of this cramped space now. He wanted to find his mother and father.

He cautiously pushed the lid to one side, and it made a clatter as it fell to the ground. He shook uncontrollably as he waited, but nothing fearful happened.

He overturned the boiler as he climbed out of it and spilled to the ground. He stood and rubbed his bruised knees. He listened a long moment before he dared advance to the door. He peered cautiously around, then shrank back at the clatter of hoofs. His eyes were dollar-big as he watched the body of horsemen ride from the settlement. He knew what they were; he had seen pictures of them, and his father had told him about Indians.

He waited a long time until he was sure the Indians were not returning, then moved slowly out of the building. He found the body of his mother first, and he ran to her. He flung himself upon her, calling to her over and over. She would not respond, no matter how much he begged. Her face was very cold, and the dried blood was all over the front of her dress. This was his first contact with death, and he struggled hard, trying to understand what had happened.

A fear was growing in his mind, a greater fear than he had ever known before. He wanted to scream against it, and his tongue was frozen, his mind paralyzed. Some instinct warned him to run, never to stop running.

He slowly backed away from the horror before

him. His father's body was a few yards farther on, but Jed did not approach it. He stood and stared, the terror in his head great drum strokes that shook him mercilessly. He turned and ran toward the woods. He only knew that he must get away from here as fast as possible. He must hide until nobody could find him again.

The few remaining Mormons filtered back from their shelter in the forest. For a while, they wandered about, a dazed, unbelieving look on their faces, their instincts numbed.

They found four wounded who needed attention. The others were all dead. They looked at each other with stunned eyes, then Meador dropped to his knees. Meador was the oldest of those remaining alive, and he took charge as his natural due. The others followed suit, dropping to their knees.

Meador prayed for a long time. He asked salvation for the dead, he prayed the Lord would loosen His most terrible vengeance upon the gentiles. In his heart, he knew what he asked for would be granted.

He stood, his face dull and stolid. "Now we must bury them," he said flatly.

Sanders was a small man, made frail by advancing age. He looked about at the dead, and his face was hopeless. "But, Henry," he said, then shut his mouth.

Meador knew what Sanders had almost said. There were so many of the dead and such a pitiful few of the living.

"We will do what we can," he said quietly. "The Lord will understand."

There wasn't really much they could do. Digging that many graves was out of the question.

"The unfinished well," Meador said.

Heads nodded dully as they understood his meaning.

The bodies were carried on a wide plank to the large, unfinished well and slid down into the gloomy hole. Meador ordered hay and straw spread over the dead, then everything was covered with a layer of dirt. The women's crying broke out then. It wasn't distressingly loud. There were so very few of them.

Meador kept them shoveling the dirt in until he was satisfied with the thickness of the covering for the bodies.

He leaned heavily on his shovel. The Dearborns had been the last two to be placed in the common grave. His face was heavy with depression. Brother Dearborn had seemed so happy here. His mouth sagged as the thought sledged into his dulled mind. There had been three of the Dearborns. Where was the boy?

He checked with everybody. Nobody had seen the boy.

"Maybe the gentiles carried him away," Sanders said.

Meador nodded in weary resignation. He had to accept that. He was helpless to do anything else.

CHAPTER 18

Doniphan's brigade was camped just outside of Richmond. Jeff had associated with many of these men for several years, and he felt the tingle of pleasure run through him at seeing them again. He wrung hands and slapped shoulders until his hand was sore. He was aware of the gleam of anticipation in their eyes at the promise of the coming campaign. War had the unfortunate ability to restore men's zest, Jeff thought soberly. It broke up the routine of the ordinary. Man was a contentious creature, and Jeff wondered if he would ever change.

Lieutenant Gladstone came up to Jeff and shook hands with him. Jeff introduced him to Turner, and Gladstone said, "I'm glad you're with us, Sheriff. We could need every man."

"What's happening, Burt?" Jeff asked.

"A constant parade of troops have passed through here, Jeff. General Atchinson marched by this afternoon with his troops from Clay and Clinton counties. General Lucas' division passed by not over two hours ago." Gladstone made a wry face. "General Lucas is an impatient man. He was pretty upset that General Doniphan wasn't already here. I heard him tell Major Powell that he expects General Doniphan to meet him on the Log Creek road not later than ten o'clock in the morning." He cocked an eyebrow at Jeff. "Do you know where that is?"

Turner spoke up. "Just outside of Richmond. We'll make it by ten and keep Lucas from biting and poisoning himself."

Gladstone didn't grin until Jeff laughed. "Sam's always been irresponsible," Jeff said. "Burt, how many troops would you say have passed through?"

Gladstone wrinkled his face in thought. "Two thousand. Maybe more. That's only from this direction."

Jeff thought he could read Turner's thoughts. Both of them remembered the day in Far West when they had watched the Mormon drill.

"It should be enough," he muttered, "to make even a hardheaded Mormon listen. I better go find out what Aleck wants to do about Lucas' order."

He found Doniphan and sat down across the fire from him. Doniphan listened thoughtfully to what Jeff reported. "That sounds like enough troops to convince the Mormons to lay down their arms without making a fight of it." He sighed.

"Getting old, Jeff. I don't look forward to battles any more."

"Then I'm getting old too, Aleck. When do you want to move out? Now or in the morning?"

Doniphan stroked his chin for a long moment, then said wearily, "In the morning, Jeff. I've been around Lucas enough recently to last me for a good while. I'd like to keep it to a minimum in the future."

Jeff looked up at the sky before he moved away. Darkness fell early these winter days. Campfires were being lit all over the bivouac area. This was going to be a long cold night.

"We could have snow, Aleck," he said.

"All we need," Doniphan said resignedly.

Doniphan was fifteen minutes late in the morning for Lucas' meeting. Jeff saw Lucas' angry look at Doniphan. He managed to keep his face frozen. No liking existed between these two. Jeff would always believe that Doniphan had been deliberate about that tardiness.

Lucas appraised Jeff and Turner. "This is a staff meeting," he snapped. "It does not include civilians."

"They're military, General," Doniphan drawled. "Both of my outfit. This is Colonel Karnes and Sergeant Turner."

"My staff meetings do not include sergeants," Lucas said coldly.

"It will, if you want to be well informed." Doniphan met Lucas head on. "There are the only two men I know of who have been in Far West. If you want to learn about the Mormons' town, you'll listen to these two."

Lucas' jaw locked hard, and temper flared in his eyes.

Jeff wondered uneasily if there was going to be an open break between the two. Lucas would have the final say-so, for he outranked Doniphan. If it came to that, Doniphan would take a spiritual mauling.

Lucas ignored Doniphan's comment and moved to a group of officers who were waiting for him. Doniphan gave Jeff a tight-lipped grin before he followed him.

Lucas' face was cold as he waited for the coughing from several officers to die down. He glared about at his listeners until he got a semblance of quiet from them. He pulled a paper from his pocket. Those cold eyes swept the group again, and Jeff had the feeling that a smug satisfaction filled Lucas.

"These are orders from Governor Boggs," Lucas said slowly. "They will be carried out." He read aloud from the paper, and his words fell like hammer blows. Boggs denounced the Mormons in the most inflammatory terms Jeff had ever heard. This sounded more like the ravings of a madman than those of a cool, dispassionate man in authority. All Mormons must be driven from the state of Missouri, or exterminated. It gave no protection to Mormon life or property.

Lucas finished reading the short, brutal order. Jeff saw the hunting gleam come into several officers' eyes. Lucas had the same gleam. If these orders were followed out, every excess would be committed upon Far West.

Atchinson broke the silence. "Surely, Governor Boggs didn't write that by himself."

Lucas misread the passion suffusing Atchinson's face. "I gave him advice and help on it."

Jeff could swear he read a smirk in Lucas' voice. He didn't dare look at Doniphan. Aleck must be close to the bursting point.

"That is the most inhuman thing I ever listened to," Atchinson said furiously. "I will not be a party to such orders."

Lucas drew himself up and looked coldly down the thin blade of his nose. "You are at liberty to leave, sir."

"Gladly, sir," Atchinson said, spun on his heel, and strode away.

"Are there any more dissenters?" Lucas asked. He saw nor heard of none. "Good. You have heard your orders. We will move on Far West tomorrow."

The meeting broke up, and Doniphan walked away with Jeff and Turner. He was seething mad. It showed in his blazing eyes, in the hard lock of his jaws.

For a moment, Jeff didn't dare break the silence.

Doniphan burst out, "The bastard. Atchinson played right into his hands. By leaving, he left Lucas with top authority."

"Do you think Lucas was hoping you'd leave too?" Jeff asked.

"I have no doubt of it," Doniphan snapped. "My God, I think he's mad. Boggs's feelings were hurt by the Mormons taking advantage of his good intentions. Lucas played on those injured feelings until Boggs gave him his way. Lucas doesn't want to put down the Mormons' minor rebellion by a show of force. He wants a war." He looked at Jeff's stunned face and said angrily, "Damn it. Can't you see? He will have won a war. It'll bring him public notice. I don't know how far up that political ladder he hopes to climb, but he thinks this will give him a few more rungs."

Jeff shook his head. "Aleck, I don't think we've got anything to say about it now. It all depends upon the Mormons and how much of a fight they want to make of it."

"Yes." Doniphan's voice was depressed. He turned and stalked away. Jeff let him go. He knew Doniphan wanted to be alone with his troubled thoughts.

CHAPTER 19

By nightfall, Lucas had established camp at Goose Creek, a mile south of Far West. He sent out scouts and established a ring of sentries around his camp. Jeff might not like the man, but as far as he could see, nothing was wrong with his ability as a soldier.

The camp covered an extensive area. Even with Atchinson and his militia gone, Jeff would estimate Lucas' force around two thousand men. Lucas also had an impressive display of artillery that he could add to horsemen and foot soldiers.

Jeff and Doniphan sat before a campfire. Neither of them had eaten with much appetite. Doniphan scowled into the flames and said, "Right now, I'd turn in my commission for a good bottle of whisky."

Jeff laughed in dour amusement. "See if you can find a second bottle for me."

Turner came up to the fire, warmed his hands, then turned his backside to the heat. "I've got some news that'll make you happy."

"I need it," Doniphan said gloomily.

"Not you, Aleck. Jeff is going to be happy to know that Nixon and his Indians just came in. He was looking damned pleased with himself."

Jeff wondered what had delayed Nixon so long,

then irritably dismissed the thoughts. He didn't give a damn what Nixon did or how.

The three sat before the fire, each silent with his own thoughts. Jeff stretched and stood. They weren't accomplishing anything by this wooden staring into a fire. "I'm getting my blankets."

Turner joined Jeff, but Doniphan shook his head. "I'm not ready yet. I'll keep the fire going awhile longer."

Three scouts rode pell-mell into camp before Jeff finished his breakfast. The first he knew anything of them was when Doniphan hurried over to him and told him about it.

"I was with Lucas when the scouts made their report. A large body of horsemen are trying to make Far West. Lucas has ordered out my brigade to intercept them. I think it's useless. By the time we're ready to ride, those horsemen will be in Far West. Want to go?"

Both Jeff and Turner nodded.

"Make it fast then," Doniphan said.

The body of horsemen hadn't reached Far West when Doniphan's brigade streamed out of the timber. Jeff saw that it was impossible to cut them off. If they wanted those horsemen, they would have to ride into Far West after them. Could those horsemen be Stacey Trenton's Danites riding back home after some marauding foray? It was entirely possible.

Jeff watched the riders enter Far West, the muscles along his jawline bunched with anger. This could be the last raid the Danites would ever go on.

Even though Doniphan was aware that he couldn't intercept those riders, he kept driving on toward the town. Anxiety grew in Jeff. He had never known Aleck to be a foolish man, but it looked as though he intended to make an assault on Far West.

Doniphan flung up an arm when he was within two hundred yards of the outskirts of town and dragged his horse to a stop.

He must have guessed Jeff's worry, for he grinned and said, "I'm not going all the way in. I just wanted to get a closer look at what we've got on our hands."

He stared at Far West for a long time, then said dryly, "They've been busy."

A line of earthen breastworks had been thrown up all around the town. "Yes," Jeff said tersely. He had seen the Mormon ability to accomplish a great amount of work in a short time. He was sorry that news of the Missouri Militia had trickled to the Mormons, but it would have been impossible to move such a great number of troops secretly. He remembered the temple foundation, dug in one day. The Mormons wouldn't have needed much time, he thought.

"That's going to make it rough," Doniphan mused.

Jeff nodded. It would, if the Mormons intended to resist.

"Look, Aleck!" Turner said in a hoarse voice.

Doniphan whipped his head back. Mounted men rode two abreast through a small gap in the earthenworks. Footmen followed them. They fanned out on either side of the gap and formed a solid front that stretched an appalling distance.

Doniphan's chuckle had no mirth. "Are they threatening us, Jeff?"

Jeff's throat felt tight. "I'd say they are, Aleck."

Doniphan scanned the Mormon formation. "About six hundred men, I'd say."

"That's close enough, Aleck."

Doniphan turned his horse. "We'd better take this news back to Lucas."

Jeff's face burned as shouted derision from the massed Mormons drifted to him. Did those damned fools think they had put Doniphan's First Missourians to flight by merely scowling at them? He looked around and saw the set, angry faces behind him. Those faces showed the same indignation he felt. These Missourians would like nothing better than to come to grips with the Mormons.

He went with Doniphan to report to Lucas. Lucas sat before a field desk inside a tent. He tapped a lower lip with a pencil as Doniphan talked.

He switched his attention to Jeff. "Colonel, do

you think you saw all the manpower they have available?"

"I think so, sir. It looked like about the same number I saw when I was in Far West."

"Do you remember the layout of the town?" At Jeff's nod, Lucas shoved a piece of paper and pencil toward him. "Sketch it," he ordered brusquely.

Jeff's eyes narrowed as he visualized Far West, then he rapidly drew a series of lines. He added a verbal description of the town and said, "I don't remember the names of the streets. From my estimation of the Mormons, I'd say we'll have to dig them out of every house, every building."

That icy hunting gleam reappeared in Lucas' eyes. "Your estimate is wrong. From the reports I've had of them, they're cowardly people, depending solely on their prayer books."

Jeff's lips pressed into a tight, thin line. Lucas was an opinionated man with no tolerance for anybody's ideas but his own. Jeff wished he had had Lucas in that blockhouse when Trenton's company made its charge to take the structure.

"If we carry the outer defenses, Colonel, will we run into more earthenworks?"

Jeff considered that at length. "I don't think so, sir," he answered slowly. "I didn't see any further defenses. I can't see how they've had enough time to construct more than the first line."

Lucas dismissed them abruptly. "That'll be all."

Baffled anger clouded Doniphan's face as he and Jeff stepped outside of the tent. "That's why he's such a popular man. He tells nobody anything."

"Your guess at what will happen, Aleck?"

"I'm saying an attack will come in the morning. Lucas is also impatient. He will not spend much time waiting."

Jeff grinned wryly. "Something to look forward to." Lucas was well prepared for an attack. He had General Parks's brigade and Robert Wilson's mounted reserves. He had more than enough artillery to flatten every structure in Far West. But Jeff couldn't get the sight of those earthen breastworks out of his mind. He knew well the Mormon determination. The Missouri Militia was going to pay a dear price to take that town.

Doniphan shook his head and said in a heavy voice, "Lucas' reputation for being bloodthirsty is well earned. He won't leave a stone unturned in Far West." He pounded a fist into his palm. "The casualties it costs to take the town won't bother him."

He tried to smile, and it was a ghastly effort. "I've got a bad feeling about tomorrow, Jeff. Pleasant thought to sleep on tonight, isn't it?"

He turned away. Jeff wondered how long it would be before Doniphan got to sleep tonight.

He found Turner piling up firewood. "We're

going to need it before the night's out," Turner said.

Jeff held back an oath. Everything seemed to be conspiring against them.

CHAPTER 20

Doniphan came to Jeff before Jeff finished breakfast in the morning. Jeff looked at that tight, grim face and tried to ask casually, "Has he ordered his attack?"

"Not yet. Three Mormons are coming in under a flag of truce. I thought you'd like to hear what they have to say."

"I'm with you," Jeff exclaimed, and bounded to his feet.

Lucas' tent was packed with his staff officers. They ringed about the three Mormons. The speaker was a stoop-shouldered, black-bearded man. He tried to meet defiantly all those probing eyes, but Jeff noticed the slight tremble to his lips. All three Mormons displayed telltale signs of nervousness. He did not blame them. If all these hostile eyes were on him, he would feel the same uneasiness.

"State your business," Lucas said brusquely.

Jeff saw an Adam's apple bob as the Mormon gulped. "Sir, I am Captain Wharton, sent at the request of Colonel Hinkle, commanding the

Caldwell Regiment. He begs a meeting with you to see if this trouble cannot be ironed out peacefully."

"Hah," Lucas ejaculated.

It was a simple word, but it expressed boundless contempt, for Wharton colored.

"Go ahead," Lucas commanded.

Jeff was surprised that Wharton had this errand instead of Trenton, then realized from the little he had seen of Trenton, this didn't fit his nature. Trenton would have nothing to do with what he would call a begging errand.

"He asks for a meeting at two this afternoon," Wharton said.

"Does he expect me to ride into Far West for this meeting?" Lucas asked sarcastically.

The flush burned deeper in Wharton's face. "No, sir," he said doggedly. "Colonel Hinkle suggests the high point of ground halfway between our town and your camp site."

Lucas' brow furrowed with thought. Jeff could guess at those thoughts. Lucas was analyzing that high point of ground as a possible ambush. He needn't worry, Jeff thought derisively. Hinkle had picked well. The meeting place was out of range of both forces.

"Granted," Lucas finally consented. "I will tolerate no trickery," he thundered. "At the first sign, you Mormons will regret it bitterly."

"Yes, sir," Wharton said tonelessly. He wheeled

and marched out of the tent, followed by his two attendants.

Lucas paced back and forth with short, jerky steps. Jeff thought sardonically, he's upset. Things haven't gone according to his plans.

Lucas stopped his pacing and stabbed a fore-finger at Jeff. "Do you know this Colonel Hinkle?"

Jeff shook his head. "If I saw him, his name wasn't mentioned to me."

Lucas thrust his head forward belligerently. "Is this some kind of a trick?"

"I don't see how it could be," Jeff replied.

"It hadn't better be," Lucas muttered. He glared about the tent. "There will be no talking about this until after the coming meeting is over. I will not have the troops speculating about it." He named six officers; Jeff and Doniphan were among them. "All of you be here by one-thirty."

"Yes, sir," Jeff said woodenly, and saluted.

Horses stomped restlessly as they waited on the high rise of ground. Their tossing heads jingled bridle chains. Lucas sat there, his wrath growing more apparent. It had been swelling ever since he found he and his staff were first at the appointed meeting place.

Doniphan glanced at Jeff, and there was amusement in his expression. Anybody who knew Lucas didn't keep him waiting.

Jeff stared at the raw scars of the breastworks.

The day was gray and cold. Several times he thought he saw movement behind the earthen fortifications, but he couldn't be sure. He felt a tingle of excitement run through him. Six men rode slowly out through the gap in the defenses.

He raised his voice. "They're coming, sir."

"It's about time," Lucas announced waspishly.

The six riders proceeded slowly until they stopped opposite Lucas and his staff. The officer leading them saluted Lucas. "General Lucas, sir? Colonel Hinkle commanding the Caldwell Regiment."

Lucas returned the salute, his eyes foreboding. "I can see nothing for us to discuss."

Hinkle's cheeks twitched. He was tall and lean, his face sunburned, the cheekbones prominent. His face was haggard with the weight of his responsibility.

"I am here to discuss a mutual agreement, General," Hinkle said. "Surely, our difficulties can be settled without war."

"There can be no agreement but one. Your unconditional surrender, Colonel."

Hinkle's lips were a tight, savage line. "General, you would pay an enormous price, if you presumed to attack."

Lucas enjoyed this brutal exchange of words. "And I point out to you, Colonel, that I have better than two thousand men in the woods behind me; plus enough artillery to level your town."

Two Americans faced each other, and each was determined to grind the other into the ground.

Lucas' face was swollen with temper. "You dare to mention cost to me? I promise you this. If I have to take your town by force, no male Mormon will be left alive." His smile had a wolfish quality. "I cannot say what would happen to your women." His inference was plain. The women would become spoils of war to a victorious army.

Hinkle seemed to wilt. "What do you demand, sir?"

Lucas pulled a piece of paper from his pocket. "These orders come from the governor. You will surrender Joseph Smith and other leaders who founded this insurrection. All arms of any kind must be given over. The Mormons, who started this rebellion, will have all their property appropriated to pay for the cost of the war and the damages they caused. Mormons not held for trial will leave the state. They will be protected until they are out of Missouri."

Jeff looked at a sick man. Hinkle had aged during Lucas' reading of the terms. His lips trembled so that he had trouble forming his words.

"My God, sir," he gasped. "You leave us nothing."

"You can refuse," Lucas said. "You know the alternative."

Hinkle stared at his folded hands on the horn. The knuckles stood out in stark relief. His voice was so low as to be almost inaudible. "I must have time to confer with my people. I ask until morning."

"Until the morning," Lucas granted. "I want Joseph Smith, Sidney Higdon, Lyman Wight, Parley Pratt, and George Robinson delivered to me. I will hold them as hostages until it is certain the governor's terms are met. I will give you an hour after sunset to produce the hostages."

Hinkle closed his eyes for a long moment. When he opened them, Jeff had the queer impression he was blind.

"Agreed," he said with the voice of an old man.

"I march on Far West an hour and a half after sunset," Lucas said relentlessly. "The only way you can stop it is by meeting my terms."

Hinkle stared at Lucas without really seeing him. "Understood," he said in faltering tones. He saluted and wheeled his mount for the mentally tortured ride back to Far West.

Lucas' face was mean with brutal satisfaction. "I knew they had no backbones. I'd hoped they'd make a fight of it."

Jeff had just seen a proud man stripped of every last vestige of his dignity. You inhuman bastard, he raged silently. Oh God, I'd like to see you in Hinkle's position. Jeff didn't have any doubt that Hinkle would submit. This was Hinkle's country. He probably knew every alien foot that trod upon it. He also knew of every item of

215

ordnance Lucas had brought here. Lucas had left a proud and sensitive man no choice but to agree to his barbaric terms.

He glanced over at Doniphan. Doniphan wore a hard, wooden mask, but the eyes were blazing. Jeff knew that Doniphan's sentiments were exactly the same as his.

CHAPTER 21

Colonel Hinkle was sick enough to vomit. He hadn't exchanged a single word with the five officers who accompanied him. They hadn't heard the intimate details of his conversation with Lucas, but by their harried expressions they suspected the worst.

Hinkle went back and forth over the meeting, trying to see a ray of light in the murky situation. He could simply refuse Lucas' terms. He could announce to the people of Far West that they would fight, and they would cheer him until they were hoarse. For a fleeting moment, a bright flame of resistance flickered, then died. He was a practical, hardheaded person, never allowing himself to be deluded by illusions. He stared at hard facts, and he realized what he faced. He had six hundred men against two thousand. That was bad enough, but Lucas had artillery with him, where he had none. Lucas could place cannon on the heights less than three hundred yards from town and pulverize the defense to dust. He did not question his troops' bravery, but against the brutal odds and superior weapons, bravery was not nearly enough.

He groaned in anguish. If he reported the actual terms, the Mormons would not accept them. They would shout down every fact, their anger rising, until they drowned out everything he said. Neither Joseph Smith nor the other leaders would listen to him. They would urge the people on, until Far West would be bathed in blood.

His desire to use his experience warred against his conscience, and his conscience won. No matter how much men screamed at him, he would not let them throw their lives away. The Lord knew what was in his heart, and that was enough to console him.

The cheers grew louder as he rode through the gap in the fortifications. Hinkle listened to the laudatory words shouted at him and was sure he was going to be ill. They believed he returned from a triumphant errand; that of warning the gentiles to stay away from Far West.

He kept his face stiffly set, shutting his ears to the shouts and avoiding all eyes. He pulled up before Joseph Smith's house, and Smith rushed out to greet him. Smith was a small unkempt little man. Ever since Smith's visitation from the Lord, he had carried a tremendous burden on his shoulders, of getting the Lord's word to the people.

"Is it all right, Colonel?" Smith asked, the tenseness in his voice making it sound brittle.

"I didn't have enough authority to complete the talk. General Lucas wants the leaders of the church to talk with him. I believe he is willing to listen to a compromise." Slowly, he named the men Lucas wanted.

Smith sighed and some of the stiffness left his face. "When does the general want this meeting?"

"This evening."

Smith's face brightened. "I agree to meet with him. But I will not weaken our stand. They must agree to many of our conditions."

Hinkle turned away like a person groping in the dark. His eyes stung. God help him now. It was done. But he could have done nothing else.

Lucas issued orders that the army would march on Far West an hour and a half after sunset. General Parks's mounted brigade would form on the right of the division as Hankers. If necessary they would go entirely around the town and attack from the rear on the first report of cannon. The cannon would signal General Graham's brigade on the extreme left. Doniphan's and Wilson's brigades formed in line of battle to the south of town. The artillery company was already moving out. That company would occupy the heights within three hundred yards of town.

Lucas watched the sun as he hurried through his final preparations. The hostages should be here by now. The sour taste of his anger filled his month. So they thought they could defy him. By God, it suited him. The blood spilling would be on the Mormon's conscience, not his.

It was almost time to move. He was leaving a few minutes early. It did not bother him.

The battle front was an awesome sight as it moved slowly out of the woods. Jeff was rather surprised that the Mormons had rejected Lucas' time limit, but my God, what else could be expected. Even a cornered rat would fight viciously when there was no way out. Lucas was going to have gaping holes in this line of battle before the conflict was very old.

Jeff peered through the deepening dusk, sure he saw movement ahead. It couldn't be the Mormons coming out from behind their breastworks, eager to join battle.

He sighed as he saw the approaching party was composed of only a few riders. A flag of truce whipped in the stiff breeze above their heads. Jeff felt the hollow of relief in his stomach.

Hinkle rode ahead of the small group. Jeff was close enough to the meeting to hear Lucas demand, "Are all the hostages here?"

"They are." Hinkle's voice was dead.

Lucas waited until the hostages reached him. He turned his head and snapped out an order.

Troops rushed forward and formed a strong guard about the Mormons. Smith turned a shocked face toward Hinkle as he realized what was happening. "You are a traitor," he whispered. His voice strengthened as deep lines of anguish etched his face. "Traitor," he screamed.

Rough hands seized the hostages and rushed them back to Lucas' camp.

Hinkle sat there, his face a death mask, incapable of seeing or hearing.

"Colonel, I will enter Far West in the morning to accept your surrender."

Hinkle nodded dazedly. He tried to say something, and the words were only a mumble. He turned his horse and rode slowly away, every action that of a sleepwalker.

Lucas briskly rubbed his hands together, and the satisfaction in his expression was sickening to see.

"I've taken their town without firing a shot," he boasted. He looked about at the rigid faces surrounding him. "Are there any of you still ready to say there is bravery among Mormons?"

He sensed much disapproval, for his mouth clamped together in that fierce slash. He touched spurs to his horse and drove forward, forcing a passage.

Jeff reined over beside Doniphan. "Damn him," he said with heat. "He should be grateful he's spending no blood. Instead—"

Doniphan cut him short. Jeff was within earshot of several officers. "I know," he said shortly. He turned back toward camp, and Jeff fell in beside him.

Doniphan shook his head at the rebellion he still saw in Jeff. "Whatever you intended to say was right and deserved. But do you want it to get back to Lucas? He's proved his pettiness. Why make the time you still must spend around him any rougher than necessary?"

Jeff blew out a hard breath. "Maybe," he said. There wasn't too much concession in the answer.

"Damn it, Jeff," Doniphan said impatiently. "Don't you think I feel the same way. Lucas is disappointed. I don't want to see him stirred up more. I'm afraid he'll try to retaliate for that disappointment."

Jeff frowned at him, not understanding at all.

"A bloody battle would have brought him much more publicity. As it is, his campaign dies quietly. He will try to punish the Mormons for that."

Jeff showed his astonishment.

Doniphan scowled. "Oh, they'll suffer. How in the hell does a small, vicious man get a position of power and authority?" He shook his head. "You heard the snide remark he made about the Mormons' bravery. What Colonel Hinkle did probably took more bravery than either of us will ever see again. Hinkle knew he risked ostracism by his own people. But he did what he knew must be done. He saved lives."

"Aleck, what's going to happen now?"

"At the best, expulsion from the state. They won't be allowed to leave with more than the clothes on their backs."

His eyebrows rose as he watched anger twist Jeff's features. "Are you surprised? Don't you realize it's only a just punishment? Can't you see they believe differently than we do. Whatever we do to them is fitting and proper."

Jeff uttered a vile oath. "And it's all done in the name of religion. Who's to blame, Aleck?"

"Mormons and gentiles," Doniphan said. "Finding out who threw the first stone isn't important."

Doniphan looked so lonely and depressed that Jeff hated to see him turn away. "Aleck, Sam will have supper ready about now. He's a hell of a field cook."

Doniphan's face brightened. "I remember some of the meals he turned out on our hunting trip. Is that an invitation?"

Jeff grinned. "You want it in writing?"

Turner was busy stirring a pot suspended over a fire when Doniphan approached him.

"Do you have enough for an uninvited guest, Sam?"

Turner displayed his pleasure. "The pot's almost full, Aleck."

Doniphan sniffed at the aroma. "It smells good."

"I put about everything I could find into it," Turner said. "I got a couple of squirrels this afternoon and traded a soldier a plug of chewing tobacco for a rabbit. I added some of the army beef, though I wouldn't vouch for that. It could be mule, or goat, or about anything else."

He dipped in the big tin spoon and tasted. "She's done." He found another tin bowl for Doniphan and ladled it full.

Doniphan tasted and said, "You're slipping, Sam. It's merely wonderful."

For several minutes, there was only the sound of eating. Doniphan refused the offer of a third bowl and patted his distended stomach. "I couldn't, Sam." He leaned back comfortably. "A meal like that almost makes a body forget his troubles."

He frowned at an approaching soldier. "I take back what I just said. This looks like trouble."

The soldier came up to him and said, "General, I've been looking all over for you. General Lucas wants you to report to his tent immediately."

Doniphan grunted in displeasure. "Tell him I'll be right along." He waited until the soldier left before he said, "Come along, Jeff. I don't know why, but my skin's crawling."

Lucas was pacing impatiently inside his tent when Doniphan and Jeff entered.

Lucas glanced coldly at Jeff but didn't comment. "General, I just concluded a meeting with my staff." At Doniphan's growing look of displeasure he said glibly, "We couldn't find you, General."

Some of the tightness left Doniphan's face. That could have been true.

"My staff and I decided that in the interest of keeping permanent peace, Joseph Smith and the other prisoners are to be executed. Take them into Far West's public square and shoot them promptly at nine o'clock in the morning."

The order stunned Jeff. He didn't dare look at Doniphan. He was sure at any instant he would hear a roar of indignation from him.

"How did you arrive at such a conclusion?" Doniphan's voice had all the chill of a January wind.

Lucas shrugged. "The rebellion was born in the minds of the ones I hold prisoner. It will be a severe lesson to others who might have kindred thoughts."

"You picked me because I was the only staff officer not present at your meeting?" Doniphan asked with ominous quietness.

Lucas shrugged again. "You are here to follow orders."

"But I don't have to follow that kind," Doniphan thundered. "It's nothing but cold-blooded murder. I march my brigade to Liberty at eight o'clock in the morning."

Lucas blanched, then a wave of red flowed into his face. "You forget I can prefer charges against you for disobeying orders."

Doniphan stabbed a finger at him. "You prefer and be damned. Execute those men, and I will hold you responsible before an earthly tribunal, so help me God."

Lucas' eyes shrank to pinpoint size and fury blazed from them. His voice was hardly audible. "Do you threaten me?"

"Be assured of it," Doniphan said grimly. "Even the governor wouldn't approve when he hears you used trickery to capture those hostages. Colonel Karnes is a witness to the entire shameful transaction."

Lucas flashed Jeff a murderous glance.

"Take good care of Colonel Karnes, General. I hold you responsible for his safety until he returns safely to Liberty."

Lucas failed to stare Doniphan down. Unbridled rage worked in Lucas' face, and it looked as though he was going into a tantrum.

Lucas licked his lips, then mumbled, "General, I never intended for you to carry out that order. I wanted Smith and the others to hear what could happen to them, if Smith still resists surrender."

"You think he could hear you from where he is," Doniphan asked contemptuously. "I'm still pulling out my brigade in the morning."

He turned and walked out of the tent. Jeff followed him. He hoped that the poison inside Lucas would keep rising until he choked on it.

Doniphan pointed to a tent, heavily guarded. A light inside the tent silhouetted the figures of men kneeling in prayer.

"Their prayers and my threat to Lucas may save them," Doniphan said dryly. "I prefer to rely on my threat."

Jeff was distressed. "Are you really leaving in the morning?"

"Lucas leaves me no alternative," Doniphan said grimly. "It's the only check I have on him. He can't be sure whose ear I will get to."

He clapped Jeff on the shoulder. "Keep an eye on him, Jeff. Lucas will make it hard on those people in Far West. You may be the only one who can keep things from becoming unbearable. I'll see you when you return to Liberty."

"I wish to God that it was tomorrow," Jeff said miserably. Jeff altered that because of Delight. But he sure wished he was riding back to Gallatin tomorrow.

CHAPTER 22

Lucas' army moved toward Far West. Doniphan's brigade was gone. Jeff and Turner had seen him off, not over a half hour ago. The gray day fit the occasion. The biting wind out of the north did nothing to lift a man's spirits. Jeff thought gloomily, Now all that's needed is for tears to fall out of the sky, to mourn this sad day. If moisture did fall, it would come as snow.

Jeff and Turner stayed well away from Lucas. Doniphan had warned Lucas to be careful of Jeff's safety, but Jeff well remembered the maniacal look he had last seen on Lucas' face. He couldn't be sure which way Lucas would jump.

Jeff's anxiety mounted. He thought surely by now he would have seen some sign of the coming surrender. It was too quiet, and he could see no movement behind the breastworks. His breathing was uneven and labored. Had Hinkle changed his mind? Did he intend to fight regardless of the hostages Lucas held?

With each forward step, Jeff's muscles drew more painfully tight. Any moment he expected fire to empty saddle after saddle and cut infantry down. Lucas still rode out in front. He wouldn't be doing that, if he expected any kind of a fight. Jeff could take weak consolation from that fact.

Lucas was nearly fifty yards from the breastworks, the others right behind him. Jeff jerked as the head logs of the breastworks suddenly tumbled outward, and white flags of surrender went up all down the line.

Jeff sighed weakly. Despite the biting chill of the day, he was sweating profusely. This campaign was officially over.

Lucas led his troops into the public square and lined them up on one side. Colonel Hinkle formed his regiment on the other side, then rode slowly toward Lucas.

The two hostile forces were less than forty yards apart. Jeff was close enough to see the spiritual beating the Mormons were taking. No woman was anywhere near the square. Jeff thought they were cowering in terror behind locked doors. He didn't see Trenton. He remembered the proud defiance in the man and thought, This surrender must be driving Trenton wild.

Hinkle saluted woodenly and slowly unbuckled his sword. Jeff had never seen a face more haggard. Hinkle's hand trembled as he drew his pistol and handed it and his sword to Lucas.

Jeff could feel the tension easing. The whooping and hollering broke out behind him and ran through the Missouri force like wildfire. Men hugged and pulled at each other. The war was over before it began.

Lucas whipped his head about and yelled fiercely at the troops. Officers worked frantically to restore order.

Lucas was furious when he finally looked back at Hinkle. "Are all your troops here?"

Jeff thought Hinkle had aged twenty years since he had last seen him. His cheeks were hollow, his eyes dull, and he shook noticeably.

"All here, sir," he replied.

"Deposit your arms," Lucas ordered.

Mormon after Mormon stepped forward and

laid down his arms. Jeff looked at a poor collection of weapons. Too many of the weapons were old, though well cared for. Many of the swords were crudely shaped out of corn knives. Hinkle had realized how poorly his troops were armed. Hinkle knew that the Mormons could have made no effective defense.

Jeff thought that only a small percentage of pistols was being turned in. A pistol was an easy thing to conceal. The hopeless despair spread among the Mormons, as man after man stepped forward to relinquish gun or sword. Trenton was nowhere in sight. Maybe Trenton hadn't yet returned to Far West, or perhaps his arrogant defiance couldn't let him take part in this surrender.

The last of the Mormons' weapons was on the ground. Lucas selected one of his companies to pick up the arms and take them away. He picked two more companies to surround the Mormons and guard them.

Only then did he look at Hinkle. "Colonel, you are dismissed," he said coldly.

Hinkle saluted for the last time, turned his horse, and slowly rode away. He was a broken man. Lucas had demeaned him in every way possible. Hinkle rode through the loosely assembled Mormons. Around him epithets and abuse rose. The soldiers he had once led now assaulted him verbally. "Traitor" and "Betrayer" were the least of the abusive words flung at him.

Jeff prayed that Lucas would dismiss the Mormons. But this was Lucas' hour of glory, and he milked it to the utmost. He held them there while the Missouri Militia marched through town. The parading seemed endless to Jeff. They wound up one street and down another, until every street had been covered. Occasionally, Jeff saw a face drawn back hastily from a window as he rode past a house.

Lucas finally dismissed the troops after an hour of parading, then ordered the Mormons off the streets. Far West seemed desolate and strangely quiet. Lucas gave no word against looting and pillaging. Without explicit orders, Jeff knew this town would be in for one night of hell.

Within an hour's time, he passed a dozen troopers, all of them in various stages of drunkenness. Those troopers couldn't have gotten their liquor in Far West.

He turned a corner as Turner came toward him. Turner showed his concern. He pointed to a group of soldiers lurching their way down the street. "Lucas doesn't intend to even try to control them, Jeff."

"No," Jeff said heatedly. Doniphan was lucky to have left when he did. He was spared the anguished embarrassment of seeing this. "Sam, I'm afraid they'll be going after the women before long."

Turner's hands bunched in impotent rage. "Oh, God damn Lucas."

"Yes," Jeff said flatly. "There's no use appealing to him to control his men. I think he'll be happy to see this town torn apart."

"Well, damn it, I'm going to do what I can," Turner said. "If I find anybody abusing Mormon women, I'll knock his goddamned head off."

"Both of us," Jeff said. The two of them couldn't do much good in trying to restore order in a town filled with drunken soldiers, but they had to do what they could. "See you later, Sam," he said as he turned away.

Turner's anger mounted steadily as he prowled street after street. Not every soldier he passed was drunk, but the percentage was enough to enrage him.

He approached two soldiers just as one of them raised a bottle to his mouth. He emptied it before Turner reached him, then tossed it into the street. The gloom of the night was thickening, and Turner didn't recognize them until he was quite close. Billings and Dexter stood on the corner. Both of them had removed their headdress.

"Look who's here," Billings jeered. "You unhappy because we didn't leave you a drink? You stick with us. Maybe we can't find you another bottle, but we can sure get you a woman."

"So you're looking for Mormon women," Turner purred. It was too dark for Billings and Dexter to notice the fury in his face.

"We sure as hell are," Billings said. His words were slurred. "After all the hell they gave us we figure we'll collect some of it back from their women."

Turner grabbed the front of their coats in each hand. He jerked them toward him, and with his superior strength raised them to their toes.

"One more word," he roared, "and I'll bash your faces in."

The pure savagery got through their veneer of drunkenness. Both of them knew from experience, when Turner was this angry, he was too much for the two of them to handle.

"Aw hell, Sam," Dexter protested. "Billings was just funning. He didn't mean—"

Turner shoved them away from him. "Get off the street. I promise you, if I see you again tonight, you'll be picking up your heads."

His wrath overwhelmed them. They exchanged frightened looks, then their eyes touched his face again before they slid away. They were more than convinced he meant what he said. They turned and slunk down the street.

Turner breathed hard. Maybe his threat would stop these two, but it wouldn't stop the others. His successful confrontation with these two didn't lighten his spirits. He hoped Jeff was having more success than he was.

He raised his coat collar and tucked his chin into it as the wind strengthened. Its bite chilled him to the bone. The air had the feel of snow in it. He couldn't remember ever having hoped for snow before, but this night he did. Snowfall would be more effective in clearing the streets than anything he and Jeff could do.

He nearly bumped into a figure stepping out of a house, and only a quick, backward step avoided the contact. The wash of faint light coming from the house enabled him to recognize this figure. He had seen that white overcoat before.

"Captain Fear Not," he said sardonically. "You missed most of the doings here today."

Trenton's eyes were glazed. For a moment, Turner thought he was drunk, then he knew that was wrong. Drinking wasn't in the Mormon religion. He suspected grief and despair put that glaze in Trenton's eyes.

Trenton panted as though he had been running. "You would never have taken the town," he said passionately, "if Hinkle hadn't betrayed us."

Turner peered at him. That wildness was akin to insanity. "He saved your lives," he said. "My God, man, don't you realize what you faced?"

Trenton made a savage slash with his hand. "We had enough force to stop anything thrown against us. All the gentiles are cowards. I have been up against one of their companies before. They did not fight."

Turner's face twisted with contempt. "You brag. You didn't get out of that encounter as well as

233

you'd like to believe. You handled a sleeping camp all right, but you didn't do a damn thing against two men in that blockhouse."

Trenton's mouth sagged. "Two men?" His voice was barely a whisper. "You're lying."

Turner grinned with cruel enjoyment. "Two," he repeated. "I was one of them." He described the terrain and how and where Mormons fell. "You didn't get up that hill, did you?"

Trenton's breathing whistled between his teeth. Turner had given him enough details to convince him that Turner had been there. "You're lying," he repeated.

Turner's grin broadened. "You know better than that. Your company couldn't take that blockhouse against just the two of us. You think that over before you do any more bragging about how cowardly the gentiles are."

He pushed by Trenton, brushing him with a shoulder. He took several steps before Trenton screamed after him, "Damn you. You'll pay for that."

Turner tried to whirl. The menace in that crazed voice was enough threat without the words. He tried to pull his gun as he turned. Without seeing it, he was sure Trenton aimed a gun at him. Something slammed into his back with the impact of a maddened bull. He felt no pain, only a shock that spread over and numbed his body. He wished he could have just one crack at that damned

Mormon. He wished— The blackness was a great wave, sweeping him along with its rush.

Jeff swore at the wind as he leaned against it. Every time he turned north, the wind battered him. He could say only one thing in its favor. The streets weren't as crowded as they had been even a half hour ago.

He felt moisture on his cheek and brushed it away. He felt more wetness as other flakes touched his face. Ah, damn it. A hard snow was all that was needed to increase the general misery in this town.

He thought he saw movement rise up from the street before him and peered more closely trying to determine what it was. Probably some drunken soldier, he thought, trying to regain his feet. He had better give him a hand before he lay out here and froze to death.

His throat tightened as he neared the figure. "Sam," he said hoarsely as he recognized Turner. Turner was inching himself along the ground, stopping every few feet, trying to raise himself.

Jeff knelt down beside him. A dark, wetly glistening spot covered too much of Turner's back.

"Sam," he begged. "What happened?"

Turner tried to grin. "Just resting, Jeff. Damned if I haven't got weak all of a sudden."

He closed his eyes, and panic rose in Jeff's

throat. There had been such an infinite weariness in Turner's eyes.

"Sam," he whispered.

Turner tried again to grin at him. "Just resting, Jeff."

"Who shot you, Sam?"

"Captain Fear Not. I was a damned fool not to check him for a gun, He shot me after I walked away from him. I guess I drove him to madness by telling him you and I stood him off that morning."

"No more, Sam." Jeff had all the information he needed. He wouldn't let Turner use more of his strength.

He straightened, his eyes harried. Turner was a heavy man, and Jeff was certain he wouldn't be able to carry him far. But Turner had to have attention. Jeff had no idea how long ago he had been shot, but he had already lost too much blood.

Three figures turned into the street, and Jeff yelled at them. There was no doubting the authority in his voice. The three soldiers hurried down the street and stopped over Turner.

"What happened to him?" one of them asked.

"Shot," Jeff said tersely. "He needs a doctor bad. Do you know where one is?"

They did and offered assistance in carrying Turner there. The distance seemed a million miles to Jeff, and he watched Turner anxiously. Turner kept closing his eyes, and it seemed longer each time before he opened them.

Turner was unconscious when they carried him into a store. A doctor sat talking and laughing to a couple of privates. This had been an easy campaign for him. He hadn't had anything to do since he had ridden in here.

Give him a job to occupy his hands, and Dr. Graham was all business. Jeff didn't dare utter a word to distract that intense, absorbed face. Graham grunted, then held up the bloody pair of forceps. "That's it," he said with satisfaction.

Jeff looked at the reddened slug, and his face hardened. He couldn't see Turner's face, for he was lying on his stomach, but his breathing was labored.

"How bad is he, Doc?"

Graham made a vague gesture that said it could go one way or the other. "He's lost a lot of blood. Ask me in the morning. If he lasts that long perhaps I can tell you."

Jeff said his thanks and strode out of the store. He could do nothing for Turner now, and he had an urgent job on his hands.

He stopped outside the building and debated upon his course. It wasn't yet ten o'clock, and a few lights were on in the town. Was Trenton still here? Trenton could have slipped out of town by now. He tried to look at it from Trenton's viewpoint. Too many people were still about, and Jeff finally concluded that Trenton would play it safe and wait for an hour when most of the town was asleep.

Jeff wanted to scream with his encroaching feeling of helplessness. If Trenton was already gone, there was no chance of tracking him down.

It was snowing hard by midnight. Jeff plodded step after step, though his legs were beginning to tremble with weariness. He had been over this town a dozen times, asking questions where he thought they would be answered. He was caught up in bitter frustration. The soldiers he asked didn't know a thing about Stacey Trenton. The few Mormons he stopped wouldn't answer him.

He drove himself on, his muscles and brain dulled by fatigue. Only an innate stubbornness kept him going. Surely, Trenton had had every opportunity to slip unseen out of town, or he could hide within it for as long as was necessary.

He turned a corner and stopped suddenly as he saw movement ahead of him in the swirling snow. Somebody was moving ahead of him, blending in with the falling snow. The solution hit Jeff with the effect of a club. Stacey Trenton had always worn a white overcoat. He could be wearing the garment now.

Jeff quickened his steps, and the weariness dropped away from him. He pulled his pistol out of his coat pocket and gripped it in his bare hand.

The figure ahead of him wasn't even aware of his presence. Jeff hurried until he was a half-dozen steps from Trenton.

He set himself and bawled, "Trenton. Stacey Trenton."

By the abrupt manner with which the figure jerked itself up short, the shouted name must have been a savage jolt. Trenton whirled, clawing frantically at his overcoat pocket.

Jeff caught no more than a sweeping glance of his face, but he had all the identification he needed. He pulled the trigger once, then again. Even though Trenton was falling, Jeff emptied a third shell into him.

He waited a long cautious moment, and there wasn't the slightest movement from the figure in the snow. He walked up to Trenton and looked down into the still face.

"That's for Sam," he said. All passion was drained out of him. My God, he couldn't be this tired.

CHAPTER 23

The smell of coffee awakened Jeff in the morning. He opened his eyes and stared stupidly about, for a moment unable to realize where he was. Then it all came back to him with a rush.

He sat up, gritting his teeth at the ache his stiffened muscles pushed through his body. Graham was awake and bending over Turner. By the looks of his drawn haggard face, he must have been awake most of the night.

Turner was asleep, but Jeff thought his color was better.

"How is he?" he whispered.

Graham rubbed his knuckles across his beard stubble. "Stronger than when you brought him in. But this isn't the best place for him to recover. He needs constant care, a woman's care."

Jeff thought of Alverna and Delight. "Would Gallatin be a better place for him? He'd get proper nursing there." At the frown forming in Graham's face, he said, "That's about twenty-five miles."

Graham pulled on his chin in reflective thought. "An army ambulance should get him there safely. If the driver doesn't try to break his neck reaching Gallatin. You come back around noon. I'll give you my decision then."

Jeff looked again at Turner before he went outside. He wished he could tell Turner about Trenton. That news would do Turner a lot of good right now.

A half-dozen men at a campfire offered him breakfast, and Jeff accepted gratefully. Last night's snow blanketed the earth. Jeff accepted it wryly. He had been in deeper snowfalls.

Two of the soldiers complained bitterly about the scantiness of the fare, but Jeff thought he was lucky to get hot coffee and fat, boiled bacon. He wondered if that bacon was Mormon or army bacon, then shrugged the curiosity away. From now on, he could be certain that Mormon supplies would make up much of the food the soldiers would be eating.

A sergeant filled Jeff's cup again and said, "Thank God, we don't have to stay here much longer."

At Jeff's puzzled look he went on, "Haven't you heard? Lucas is planning to take the prisoners to Independence as soon as he can. General Clark is due to arrive here tomorrow with new troops to relieve Lucas. Clark is going to take over the guarding of the Mormons." He spat into the fire, cocking his head to hear it sizzle. "I'll be glad to get out of here. Haven't you seen how these Mormons look at us. I think they'd like nothing better than to cut our throats."

"Probably," Jeff said soberly. He felt no criticism of the Mormons. If the positions were reversed, the sergeant would feel as the Mormons did. About all a beaten man had left was his sullen hatred.

He thanked the sergeant for his breakfast and strolled about town. He stayed well away from Lucas' headquarters. He and the general made no attempt to hide their contempt for each other. He was lonely. With Doniphan gone and Turner incapacitated, Jeff felt as though he didn't have a friend left in the world. He wished he was on his way back to Gallatin. He couldn't do anything for the Mormons, but he had made a promise to Doniphan, which he would keep. He grinned ruefully. Doniphan had a knack of extracting those kind of promises.

He went back to talk to Turner before noon. Turner's color was much better, and though some of the brightness in his eyes might be fever-induced, he sounded rational enough.

"How are you feeling, Sam?"

"I'm not up to running a race," Turner grunted. "But I'll make it."

"You caused me a little concern, Sam."

"I caused myself some, Jeff. I don't remember too much about last night, after I was hit. Did I make any sense?"

"Enough, Sam. You told me about Captain Fear Not."

The name brought a twist of pain to Turner's face. "That bastard," he said softly. "I'm sorry I didn't have a crack at him. He got me in the back. I was careless not checking him for weapons, but I thought all guns had been turned in." He muttered an oath. "I know better than that. I imagine he's slipped out of town by now." He sighed regretfully. "Oh well—" He let the rest of it trail away.

"He can't slip very far, Sam."

Turner's eyes widened. "So you ran him down. I might have known."

"Yes." The clipped word told Turner every-thing he needed to know.

"I won't try to thank you, Jeff."

The silence between them was comfortable, and they both enjoyed it. Jeff broke it by saying, "Sam, the doctor thinks it'd be best for you to be sent home. He'll send you back in an ambulance."

Turner started to protest, then stopped and said, "Guess there's nothing more I can do here. When are we leaving?"

"I'm not going now, Sam. I promised Aleck I would stick around to see how things are going."

Turner opened his mouth, and Jeff cut him off. "Do you think I'm going to enjoy it? You tell Delight I'll be along as soon as I can."

Jeff had seen two departures and an arrival in less than a day. He had seen Turner off yesterday afternoon and had given the driver a final admonition, "You take it easy."

Later that afternoon, General Clark, with his army, had marched into Far West. Jeff watched the greeting between Lucas and Clark. It seemed more than cordial, and he groaned, "Oh God, not another mentality like Lucas'." Jeff pondered long over the exchange of general officers, and his inability to come up with an answer bothered him. It seemed such a waste of time and manpower.

The answer began to come to him as he watched Lucas leave for Independence, Missouri.

He took a hundred prisoners with him, and that raised the boiling point of Jeff's blood. The majority of those prisoners were just little men, acting under church orders. Lucas had collected all of the important leaders before he threw in more prisoners. Jeff began to understand Clark's reason for coming here. Lucas wanted to get out of Far West; he had wrung all the glory he could out of the town. Now he marched off in search of more in Independence. Those prisoners would never get a fair trial in a town where they had had so much prior trouble.

Jeff's eyes smoldered as the companies left Far West. Lucas was gone. Jeff thought he could leave now, but Doniphan would want a thorough report of what happened to Far West. Jeff groaned. He would have to stay a few days longer to see the final windup of the Mormon town.

Nixon's company left with Lucas. Nixon wouldn't mind all those miles to Independence. He would enjoy the attention they would get in delivering the prisoners. He would like the hooting and shouted derision at the shambling men in the street. Nixon and Lucas, Jeff thought in black anger. They're two of a kind; only the rank is different.

Jeff tried to see Clark, but a staff officer deftly turned him aside. Jeff's cheeks were tight as he walked away. He had no standing of any kind at headquarters any more. He speculated upon what kind of a man General John Clark was. Clark came from Howard County, but Jeff had never met him. But surely, Clark had to be of a different caliber from Lucas. The Mormons would surely be allowed to leave the town to cut firewood and take in some of their unharvested crops.

At the end of three days, Jeff's rage had risen until he choked on it. Clark wasn't any better than Lucas. He wouldn't allow a Mormon to leave town for any reason. A new snowfall blanketed the earth. Only the tracks of wild animals broke its surface outside of town. Inside, human and animal feet churned the snow into a dirty slush, until Jeff cursed every step he took.

He couldn't believe what was happening. If anything, Clark was screwing a more vicious clamp down on the Mormons than Lucas had done. The temperature was beginning to plummet, dropping into the teens at night. For people in unheated houses, that meant real suffering. Clark and his officers had taken over two buildings, and those buildings were heated. The troops huddled around the campfires. Jeff watched this development with sick disgust. There had to be some purpose behind this cruel and unnecessary punishment. Jeff was glad that Colonel Hinkle hadn't seen this. Hinkle had trusted in a soldier's honor. In Lucas and Clark there was no such thing. The Mormons were cold and hungry, and

Jeff felt there was a deliberate purpose behind the imposed suffering.

Every time Jeff passed a Mormon woman with her face pinched from hunger and blue with cold, he wanted to tear at Missouri authority until he shredded it. The sight of the children affected him even more. He didn't see a one of them that didn't have a runny nose, and all of them moved apathetically.

To worsen matters, a company of soldiers straggled down the street, carrying meat from butchered mutton and beef.

Jeff wanted to beat hell out of them. The Mormons were starving, and food they had raised was all around them. This damned army under Clark was stealing everything they had.

He whirled and strode toward headquarters. This time, Clark was going to talk to him.

A lieutenant blocked his passage, and at every request Jeff made, shook his head. He must have read the intention in Jeff's face, for before Jeff shoved him aside, he called over two guards.

Jeff realized he couldn't get by these three men. He forced a lid on his spewing anger. He would do no one any good if he was arrested.

In the morning, he found out what Clark had in mind. Clark ordered a public assembly in the square. The Mormons looked alike now, just dead eyes in sunken faces carved from stone. He contrasted the vitality, the drive he had known in these people before. He wondered who was behind this fiendish scheme, Boggs or Lucas. Whoever it was should be satisfied now. These were crushed people gathered here.

Clark kept them waiting a half hour in the cold. He finally rode into the square and pulled up before the waiting people. He stared at them a long moment before he spoke. Jeff doubted there was the slightest pity in him. Then he realized all of this suffering was part of a harsh purpose. Clark was sent here to put the final pressure on the Mormons, to grind them down until the last spark of resistance was stamped out.

Clark raised his voice and read from a piece of paper. "You have lost your leaders and your arms. Now you must sign over all your property to defray the expenses of the war. When you do, you will be allowed to go into your fields to obtain food and wood. In a few weeks, you must leave the state forever. If you do not sign, you will stay here and starve."

He tried to look sad, and the fraud of the expression made Jeff ill. "I hurt to see you people suffering like this. Your false leaders misled you. They fastened chains of superstition about you. How I wish I could deliver you from the fetters of the fanaticism they built. But that deliverance rests with you. I advise you to scatter when you leave here and never again organize with bishops."

Jeff thought he would vomit in the street. This

damned hypocrite didn't mean anything he said, unless it was the one forecasting the expulsion of the Mormons. Clark didn't give a damn what happened to any of them. Jeff wanted to rave at him until he thought he would burst. What else could the Mormons do but sign over their property. They had hungry women and children.

If revulsion would kill a man, Clark would have dropped dead. Clark must have felt the impact of Jeff's eyes, for as he left the square, he turned his head and stared long at Jeff.

Jeff was weak with frustration. He wished he could point out the politician that was behind all this. After the Mormons signed, a lot of land was going to be up for grabs. Jeff could bet the little, ordinary man would never get his hands on any of it.

The Mormons broke up into little segments to talk over Clark's speech. This new blow was the one that crushed them hopelessly. They'd sign; they had to, or starve.

Jeff turned toward Rowdy. He saw no sense in staying here an hour longer. He didn't know how long it would take to write the final, shameful page, but Doniphan would have his report. Doniphan was a lawyer. But even then, Jeff doubted he could do anything about this rotten steal. A lone lawyer could do little or nothing against an array of politicians.

He mounted and rode away, pausing at the

outskirts of Far West to glance back. He tried to visualize it as Harmon, the bishop he had talked to, had proudly described it. He could see nothing of that vision. He felt a vast emptiness inside.

He turned Rowdy toward Gallatin. "It could have been," he muttered. "If man wasn't born with that cussed streak of meanness." He wasn't so sure that God was winning the never-ending conflict between himself and the devil. Satan had shown a lot of power here.

CHAPTER 24

Delight saw Jeff coming before he reached the house. She flew out of the door and ran toward him, her arms wide. She was laughing, but there was suspicious moisture in her eyes. She threw her arms about his neck and covered his face with kisses. He caught her face between his hands to hold it still. His own eyes stung as he bent his head to kiss her.

When he lifted his head, there was no doubt about the tears in her eyes. "I worried so much about you," she whispered.

"There wasn't any reason," he said softly.

"Wasn't there?" she retorted. "Sam was shot."

The sight of her wiped everything else out of his mind. He hadn't even thought to ask about Turner.

"How is he, Delight?"

"Better. He's getting crankier every day." The impudence showed in her smile again.

He laughed in relief. "That's good to hear." He bent his head to kiss her again, and she deftly avoided his lips.

"Not out here where everybody can see us," she murmured.

That drew another laugh from him. That hadn't bothered her when she first ran to him, but he wasn't complaining. No question had been asked, nor any answer passed between them, but both of them knew they were bound to each other as completely as a man-made covenant could make them.

She tucked her hand under his arm and fell into stride with him as they walked toward the house. Alverna waited for them at the door. Jeff sighed in regret. It seemed as though the world was conspiring to see that he had no more private moments with Delight. He might as well see Turner and get it over with. Alverna and Delight, too, would like to hear what happened in Far West.

They climbed the steps, and Jeff said from the door, "Is lying around all you have to do?"

Turner couldn't keep the pleasure out of his expression, but he said caustically enough, "Did you finally get your vacation out?"

Jeff smiled at Delight. "You were right about that crankiness. Is he like this every day?"

That impish gleam was back in her eyes. "This is one of his better days."

Jeff walked over to the bed, hand extended. "How are you doing, Sam?"

Turner didn't have the old power in his grip, but his color was good, his eyes bright.

"As well as could be expected with the lack of attention I get around here." Turner grinned at the face Delight made at him.

"How did it go at Far West, Jeff?"

Jeff soberly related everything that had happened. "It made me sick to watch, Sam. I don't know who first started it, but then, it got completely out of hand until the politicians stepped in and took over. It wound up with the helpless people being stripped of everything. The politicians will think of some high-sounding words to justify their actions, but underneath it was pure thievery."

Turner was silent a moment. "You don't think anybody will try to help them?"

Jeff shook his head. "Not a chance. They made the mistake of being on the weakest side. That's an unforgivable sin."

Turner picked at the design in the quilt. "At first, I thought it was just a simple matter of men breaking the law and being punished for it. It went far beyond that, didn't it?"

"Far beyond," Jeff agreed. He looked at Delight. "I could use something to eat." Maybe that would get him a few more private minutes with her.

She regarded him with grave attention, but warm color was suffusing her face. "We might be able to do something about that."

He followed her into the kitchen and swept her into his arms. He lifted his head and murmured, "It's been a hundred years since I've seen you."

"I know," she whispered. She suddenly pushed at him. "Mother's coming."

He wanted to swear. The world with other people in it was going to be a tough one to live in.

To ease the growing frown on his face, Delight said, "It's your fault. You said something about wanting to eat. She only came down to help."

He laughed ruefully. "I always talk too much for my own good."

Alverna insisted they be seated while she prepared food. Jeff sat across from Delight. He could revel in looking at her, but that didn't answer all of his needs.

Something troubled her, for he saw the shadow in her eyes. "What is it, Delight?"

She took a deep breath, then her words rushed out. "Jeff, do you remember Jed? The little Mormon boy?" At his hesitation, she said impatiently, "You helped his father with his wagon."

She went on after Jeff's nod. "The Haines' found him several days ago wandering in the woods. Ross said he had an awful time subduing the child. He was wild with terror, and he fought Ross like an animal."

Jeff's frown increased. Something was all wrong. "Go on," he said.

"They took Jed home. He's better now, quieter and under control, but Sarah says he breaks into screams at night."

Jeff reached across the table and captured her hand. He could feel her trembling. "Do you know what's bothering him? Where are his parents?"

"I've talked to him, Jeff. He remembered me." Delight took a deep breath to steady her voice. "He says his parents are dead." She stared at him wide-eyed as though she dreaded to say her next words. "Jeff, Jed says they were killed by Indians. I thought maybe some terror had twisted his mind, but he insists he saw those Indians."

Jeff's face had a stonelike quality. A child's terrified babbling might result in clearing up some puzzling things. The only Indians he knew of in this country were Nixon's Amaraguns. Maybe this was the explanation of why Nixon was so tardy in joining Lucas. Maybe Indians had raided that settlement.

He frowned as he asked, "Delight, do you remember the name of the place Dearborn was trying to reach?"

"Haun's Mill," she replied.

"That's it," he said, and stood.

Dread was in her face as she asked, "You're going to see if what Jed said could be true?"

"I am."

253

"I knew you would," she said miserably. "I almost didn't tell you about it for fear of this."

Alverna came in from the kitchen. "Will you settle for cold meat, Jeff?"

He looked at the cold, sliced meat and smelled the aroma of fresh-baked bread. His stomach rumbled.

"Just a sandwich, Alverna. I've got something to do. Delight will tell you all about it."

He waited for his sandwich, picked it up, and started for the door.

Delight blocked his way. "You'll be careful, Jeff?" she whispered.

He brushed her forehead with his lips. "With you waiting for me, I'd be a damned fool not to be careful. I'm coming back."

It hadn't been difficult finding Haun's Mill. From a distance, the tiny settlement looked peaceful enough, but Jeff frowned. It had some quality he couldn't name. He only knew that he felt uncomfortable here. He slowly scanned the buildings. The ominous feeling grew. He didn't see a single plume of smoke from any of the chimneys, and this day was too cold without heat.

He moved Rowdy forward slowly, his senses alert. This place was too peaceful. He didn't hear a sound, and he tried to analyze what he felt. Haun's Mill had a haunted aura, and it grated on his nerves. He stopped at the first house and called out. He couldn't believe that a silence could have this much impact.

He swung down and went into the house. This house had been pillaged, and evidence of rough ransackers' hands was everywhere. Furniture was overturned and broken, and bed-clothing was torn and strewn through the rooms.

It was the same in every house he entered. The ransackers hadn't missed a one. In several, he found dried splotches of blood, showing where somebody had died, or bled in a futile effort to stop the looters.

The dried blood in the blacksmith shop showed where a group of men had made their stand. Their stand had been no more successful here than the ones made in the houses.

Jeff scowled about at the brooding silence. Now he could understand the eerie feeling he had, as he entered this settlement.

He started to ride out when the large, unfinished well drew his attention. He swung down and walked up to it. He stood at its lip, peering down into the well. The snow hadn't covered all the dirt, and he saw the heaped-up mound. He had dug a few wells himself, and this was an odd way to go about digging one. It looked as though this well had been dug much deeper, then refilled. The dirt in the middle of it was loose.

He shivered and couldn't say why. The wind was sharp, but a moment before he hadn't felt this numbing chill. He felt a sadness, comprised of all the suffering and misery in the world, envelop him. He stared at the well, shuddered, then turned and hurried back to Rowdy.

He rode for a long way unseeing. He thought he could safely guess what had happened back there. With Lucas' march upon Far West, Nixon thought that all restraints had been loosened on him. He had attacked Haun's Mill in retaliation for Trenton's mauling of his company. Jeff gritted his teeth. He would probably never find out how Jed escaped that massacre, but there was no doubt in Jeff's mind that Jed had seen the marauders.

He headed back toward Gallatin. He had no idea when Nixon would return from Independence. No matter how long it took, he would wait.

He passed that shabby, run-down house, then checked Rowdy. Turner had pointed out the house to Jeff as the one owned by Nobby Owens. Smoke trailed from the chimney. Nixon had returned; at least Nobby was home.

He dismounted and walked to the door. He knocked on it with deceptive softness. He wanted nothing to alarm his quarry.

Owens opened the door, his eyes widening at the sight of Jeff. His stammering showed how ill at ease he was. He didn't quite know what to say.

"Just get back, Nobby?" Jeff asked softly.

Owens' eyes slid over his face. Karnes didn't

mean him any harm; at least, he didn't sound like it. "Why yes," he said uncertainly. "Just a few hours ago. I told Nixon and Inman that I'd drop off here and join them in town later."

Jeff hit him in the chest; the blow so completely unexpected that Owens had no time to set against it. It slammed him across the room and into a wall. He hit it with enough force to make the wall creak and groan.

Jeff was on him before Owens could slide down to the floor. He gripped Owens' coat at the neck and jerked him back to his feet. With the other hand, he slapped Owens methodically and mercilessly.

Owens clawed at the wrist holding him against the wall. He tried to talk, and the slapping broke up his words, rocking his head from side to side. His outrage quickly faded to a whimpering, then into an open blubbering.

Jeff stopped hitting him long enough to ask, "Do you want to tell me about Haun's Mill, Nobby?"

He didn't miss the terrified flicker in Owens' eyes before he quavered, "I don't know what—"

Jeff slapped him again, this time with more force, for the sound was loud in the still room. "I can keep this up for the rest of the day, Nobby. Can you take it? Nixon's Amaraguns raided Haun's Mill, didn't they? You were there when they massacred the Mormons, weren't you?"

"No, no," Owens moaned. Tears ran down his reddened cheeks in a steady flow. "I don't know what you're talking about."

Jeff slapped him again. "Then you better learn in a hurry, Nobby. Otherwise, I'm going to beat your head off."

Without Jeff's support, Owens would have fallen. "Make your choice, Nobby. I don't give a damn which way it goes."

Owens caved in all at once. "I didn't want to do it," he moaned. "But Mace insisted. He said we owed those Mormons that."

Jeff opened his hand, and Owens fell to the floor. "Keep on talking."

"Mace shot a man coming out of a small building. When a woman followed him, Mace shot her too."

That sounded like Jed's parents. "A pregnant woman?"

Owens gestured helplessly. "I guess so. Mace said she wouldn't raise any more Mormons."

Jeff had to struggle to keep from kicking this groveling wreck.

Owens read the disgust in his face and bleated, "I didn't shoot either of them. I didn't."

"Maybe not those two," Jeff said remorselessly. "But you took part in killing the others. If you're real smart, Nobby, you'll get out of this country as fast as you can. When some of the decent people hear about this, they'll want to talk to you too."

He turned and walked to the door. Owens' begging call didn't turn him. He doubted if his last threat to Nobby was true. The people around here had no sympathy for the Mormons. Jeff doubted seriously that any jury would find Owens guilty. That was symbolic of the sickness that gripped this country. He was afraid it would take a long passage of time before people again thought rationally.

He mounted and rode toward town, going over and over his coming confrontation with Nixon. All he had was Owens' testimony. That wouldn't stand up, if Nixon kept his head and denied everything Owens said. Jeff's teeth were set so hard that his jaws ached. He wasn't going to let it stop here; he just didn't quite know what to do about getting Nixon's part in the massacre out in the open.

He found Nixon's and Inman's horses tied up to Dexter's hitch rack. How well he remembered the two animals from the day he had stopped Nixon and Inman from manhandling Dearborn. He didn't care how much business Dexter had. Jeff wanted to break Nixon before as many people as possible.

He walked into the saloon. Nixon and Inman were among a half-dozen men leaning against the bar. Nixon was the center of attention. He said something, threw back his head, and roared with laughter. Everybody joined in his mirth.

Jeff put his gun in his outside coat pocket. He looked at a bleak picture in his mind without shrinking. He was going to kill a man.

He didn't know how many men in the room belonged to Nixon's company, and he didn't care about that, either. His fury was a cold, bright-burning flame that devoured all ordinary thoughts.

He walked to a spot a dozen feet behind Nixon and stopped.

Dexter saw him first, and he must have read the menace in him, for his hands were arrested in midair and a nerve twitched in his cheek.

"What are you going to do now, Mace?" Jeff asked in a deceptively soft tone. "Now that the Mormons are gone, where are you going to get your women and children to kill?"

Nixon heard him all right, but he hesitated a long moment before he whirled. Jeff's question must have momentarily frozen his reflexes.

He stared at Jeff, breathing unevenly. The tightening skin on his face made his cheekbones stand out prominently. "I don't know what you're talking about," he blustered.

"Oh yes, you do," Jeff said, his voice brittlely cold. "How many did you kill at Haun's Mill? You were able to slip up pretty close in that timber before they even knew you were there. Did you enjoy massacring the women and children as well as the men?"

Dexter's face turned a doughy gray. He sidled

away from behind Nixon. Inman gasped audibly. Jeff didn't see the shocked reaction in the others' faces.

Men began moving away from Nixon, covering a surreptitious inch at a time. Nixon looked as though he couldn't form his words, for he kept licking his lips.

"You're crazy," he said, and attempted a shaky laugh.

"You know better than that, Mace," Jeff said. "Nobby told me all about it."

That jolted Nixon hard, for the break in his breathing could be heard. "He's a damned liar," he said hoarsely.

"You named the wrong one, Mace. You remember the Mormon you were beating when Delight and I came up that day. He had a pregnant wife and a little boy. You should have killed the little boy too. He saw you and your Indians. You killed his father and mother."

Nixon's face was a ghastly white, and his frantic eyes said that he was close to the breaking point.

"Mormons," he screamed. "Damned, worthless Mormons. Everybody around here is just as happy they're all dead."

"Look at them, Mace," Jeff said. "They didn't hate as deeply as you do. They didn't want to kill mothers and children."

Nixon glanced uncertainly about him. He read the judgment in the faces about him. Jeff had called it right. Revulsion was written on most of the faces. Hating was a man's business; it didn't include women and children.

Nixon found himself judged and wanting. His nerves shattered at the silent accusation he saw all around him.

"Damn you," he screamed, and clawed for his gun. His desperate need for haste made him ineffective. Jeff drew and fired before Nixon got his gun out.

One shot was all that was needed. Jeff looked at the crumpled figure on the floor. Hate was still stamped on that still face. Perhaps fear was mixed in with the hatred.

He raised his head and glanced slowly about the room. Most of the eyes wouldn't meet his. Inman and Dexter had no desire to carry on Nixon's fight. They wouldn't even raise their heads.

Two other men met Jeff's eyes and nodded a slow understanding. The shame in their eyes replaced all the censure that had once been there.

Jeff walked to the door. He would be glad to get the sour taste of Gallatin out of his mouth. It hadn't brought him much but misery. That wasn't right at all, and he changed it. He had found Delight here.